The Dante Inferno:

Luc's Unwilling Wife

The Dante Dynasty Series:
Book #5

by

Day Leclaire

USA Today Bestselling Author

Please Note

This is a work of fiction. Names, characters, places, and incidents either are the product of the author's imagination or are used fictitiously, and any resemblance to actual persons, living or dead, business establishments, events or locales is entirely coincidental.

Cover Design by Melyssa Naujoks, 2019

For more information, please visit my website:

http://www.DayLeclaire.com

Book Description

Her Inferno Bodyguard... Dantes' security chief, Luc Dante is coerced into six weeks of protection duty for heiress Téa de Luca—just until she reaches her twenty-fifth birthday and can claim her inheritance. The job should be a snap for the powerful, former Special Forces tough guy, despite a wound that never properly healed. After all, who would want to harm such a brilliant, family-oriented woman? Only two things stand in his way...

First, Téa is the most adorable, gorgeous, sexy— *annoyingly oblivious*—person he's ever met, ready and blithely willing to tumble headlong into any and all disasters that appear in front of her. Not that she sees them.

And second, there's the small matter of The Inferno, which strikes the second they touch. Of course, that one touch leads to another. And then another and another until they find themselves tumbling into a disaster to end all disasters ... the nearest bed. Maybe it wouldn't have been so bad if they hadn't been caught in the act. Bound by an unbreakable Dante code of honor, their next disastrous step is to the altar.

What neither realizes is there's a very good reason Téa needs a bodyguard. And if they don't see what's happening right in front of them, even The Inferno won't be enough to save them.

Dedication

To Kathy Jorgensen, my sister in spirit.

Table of Contents

Book Description iv

Dedication.. vi

Other Titles by Day Leclaire viii

Prologue 9

Chapter One... 15

Chapter Two... 34

Chapter Three 57

Chapter Four.. 82

Chapter Five.. 103

Chapter Six 128

Chapter Seven 151

Chapter Eight... 174

Chapter Nine.. 195

Chapter Ten 214

Epilogue 239

Meet Day Leclaire 243

Other Titles by Day Leclaire

The Dante Inferno:
The Dante Dynasty Series

*Some blazes, once ignited, can't be extinguished. Just one burning touch connects a Dante with his soul mate.
The Inferno ... curse or blessing?*

Sev's Blackmailed Bride, Book #1

Marco's Stolen Wife, Book #2

Nicolò's Wedding Deception, Book #3

Lazz's Contract Marriage, Book #4

Luc's Unwilling Wife, Book #5

Rafe's Temporary Fiancée, Book #6

Draco's Marriage Pact, Book #7

Gianna's Honor-Bound Husband, Book #8

Becoming Dante: Gabe, Book #9

Dante's Dilemma: Romero, Book #10

Forever Dante: Lucia, Book #11

Prologue

"I need your help."

If it had been anyone other than his grandmother uttering those words, Luc Dante would have walked away. But coming from a woman he loved with all his heart, he found himself replying, "What can I do?"

Beautiful hazel eyes, wise with the weight of her years, held a wealth of compassion, as well as a twinkling of the irrepressible humor that defined her character. She hesitated just long enough for a faint warning bell to sound, an internal alarm he'd long ago learned to listen for and respond to with all due haste.

"The truth is, it is a friend of mine who needs your help," she admitted.

"Nonna—"

"Hear me out, Luciano." In her own way, his grandmother could be as autocratic as his grandfather, Primo. At his nod, she continued. "You remember my dear friend Marietta de Luca, do you not? We all vacationed together one summer at the cabin when you were a boy.

You children all called her Madam. Even her grandchildren address her by that name."

It took a moment to summon the memory from his childhood. Then it popped into crisp focus. The Dante family summer home. The lake. His three brothers, sister, and four cousins all running rampant. And three little girls—Madam de Luca's grandchildren—with frizzy black hair and pitch eyes whom they'd secretly dubbed the three witches.

There'd been a fourth girl, he recalled, with bright red hair, white, white skin and intense eyes, who'd drifted from shadow to shadow and rarely spoke. Most of the time, she had a nose in a book. Showing stunning originality, they'd dubbed her Red.

Even more oddly, she made him itch. It was the only way he could describe it, that vague jittery reaction he had whenever she came too close. It made him want to poke at her, to try to elicit a reaction. But she'd shied away from all of them, vanishing like a ghost whenever they approached, showing up at mealtimes long enough to nibble at her food before slipping away again. For some reason, her behavior had irritated him. He might have done something about it, if not for the watchful eye of his grandparents.

Luc shook off the memory. "I remember Madam," he admitted. He also remembered thinking it would make the perfect name for a dog, but decided—even at such a tender age—it might be wise to keep that particular tidbit to himself. A brief image flashed through his head of an elegant, aristocratic woman with coloring to match her dark-haired grandchildren, a woman who could command obedience with a single black look. "What about her?"

"Her eldest granddaughter, Téa, needs your assistance for a few weeks."

He wondered briefly which of the witches was Téa, but the bell inside his head sounded another warning, this one louder than before and he focused on that, instead. "What sort of assistance?" he asked suspiciously.

"Well . . ." Nonna released her breath in a sigh. "To be honest, she needs a bodyguard."

Luc shot to his feet, his knee screaming in protest at the unexpected jolt. *Damn it to hell!* "No."

"Now, Luciano—"

He limped to the bank of windows of Dantes conference room where his grandmother had cornered him and stared out at the city of San Francisco. Any other day, he'd have admired the crystal clear spring morning which offered a stunning view of San Francisco Bay, along with a startling backwash from a crisp blue sky. Not today. Not this moment. Not when memories tried to crowd their way into his thoughts and heart.

"I can't." The words came out far harsher than he'd intended. "Don't ask me to go through that again."

"It was not your fault," Nonna said quietly.

He pivoted on his good leg, struggling to hold the nightmare at bay. But flashes crept through, no matter how hard he worked to keep them compartmentalized. The urgent rush to escape their pursuers. The SUV coming out of nowhere. The car crash. The child. Oh, God, the child. The husband, gone. The wife, broken. The sound of her weeping. Her pathetic pleas.

"Let me die! Just let me die so I can be with them!"

He closed his eyes and forced the memories into the furthest recesses of his mind. "I can't do it, Nonna. I won't."

"It is not that sort of job," she said with such gentleness it threatened to overwhelm him.

He waited until he regained his self-control. "It is that sort of job if I need to guard her," he corrected with amazing calm.

"Attend to me, *cucciolo mio*. Téa is to receive a large inheritance when she turns twenty-five." Nonna raised her eyes to the heavens in clear benediction. *"If* she turns twenty-five."

Facts first. Refuse later. "Someone wants to prevent that from happening?"

"No, no. Nothing like that. Téa is . . ." Nonna made a tsking sound with her tongue and then switched to Italian. *"Ignaro.* Oblivious. The girl is highly focused."

Luc lifted an eyebrow and followed suit, switching to Italian. "Which is it? Oblivious or focused?"

Nonna gave a speaking shrug. "Both. She is very organized and focused on that which holds her attention. Such organization and attention to detail causes her to be somewhat oblivious to all else. It has gotten to the point where she has become seriously accident prone."

"So, lock her up in a room somewhere for—" He tilted his head to one side. "How long?"

"Six weeks."

"For six weeks."

"First, the de Lucas would have to get her to agree, which she will not. Secondly, she is the main support of her family. She cannot afford to take a six-week leave of absence. They are in serious financial straits."

"Why does that change when . . . Téa?" He lifted an eyebrow and at his grandmother's nod, he continued. "When Téa turns twenty-five?"

"On her next birthday, she receives a huge trust fund and ownership in a business which will support the entire family for the rest of their lives. If she does not—" Nonna shrugged again. "The money does not."

"I already have a job."

And he did. Sort of. As head of security for Dantes Courier Service, the branch of the business that handled the day-to-day operations of safely transporting Dantes fabulous fire diamonds, gemstones, and jewelry, he wouldn't normally have time for this. But after a recent robbery of one of the shipments the police and insurance company were investigating, and DCS had been temporarily shut down.

Nonna's eyes flashed with hazel fire. "Do not insult my intelligence."

Luc sighed, hearing the painful snap of the trap closing around him. "Let me get this straight. You want me to safeguard a klutz so she makes it to her twenty-fifth birthday? That's it? No danger. No actual bodyguarding? You just want a what? A babysitter?"

Nonna smiled in relief. "Exactly. Téa needs a babysitter for the next six weeks and I promised Madam you would sit on her baby."

Chapter One

Luc lounged—as best as a six-foot three-inch man could lounge—in the dainty chair at the small bistro table outside a trendy downtown San Francisco restaurant. He struggled to control his impatience. Beside him Nonna and Madam chatted happily in Italian while they awaited the arrival of Téa de Luca, or Witch Girl #1 as Luc had privately dubbed her. Because she was late, a trait that—quite literally—drove him out of his ever-loving mind, he was in hurry up and wait mode, one of his least favorite memories of his military service.

It was rude. It was self-indulgent. And it gave the underlying message, "It's all about me." He despised women who adopted that sort of attitude and avoided them like the proverbial plague.

He reached for a breadstick and pulverized it between his teeth. Where the hell was she? It wasn't like he had all day to sit around waiting on Her Witchiness. Well, actually, he supposed he did now that he was temporarily out of a job while the cops and insurance company looked into the fire diamond heist. But there were plenty of other things he'd rather do. Like drive a spike between his ears, or tie himself to a railroad track in front of an oncoming freight train, or swim with a pack of voracious Great White sharks.

He cleared his throat and leaned toward Madam. "Where the he—" He broke off beneath the withering glare emanating from his grandmother and rethought his choice of words. "Would you mind trying Téa's cell again, Madam?"

"Do you have another appointment, Luciano?" Nonna asked. Her tone came across sweet enough, but a hint of hazel fire flashed through her eyes. A warning message he pretended not to notice.

"As a matter of fact, I do," he lied without remorse.

Madam picked up the pretty lavender cell phone she'd set on the table as gingerly as if it were a landmine. Peering through a pair of reading glasses hanging from a crystal beaded necklace around her neck, she carefully punched in a number. "No, no. That's not right," she murmured, her brow furrowing.

"I think if you just hit send several times it dials the last number," Nonna explained helpfully.

"Would you like me to take care of it?" Luc offered.

Madam passed him the cell with an amusing combination of relief and hauteur, reminding him again why she'd been given her particular moniker. "If you wouldn't mind, I would appreciate it."

"Happy to help."

He pushed the speed dial and waited for the call to connect. While it rang he automatically scanned the busy sidewalk just past the frilly, wrought iron fence that separated the outdoor section of the café from the rest of humanity. It was an occupational hazard he'd developed first during his military career, and then when he'd opened his own personal security business. And it had spilled over into his current—he grimaced—or rather former job as head of security for Dantes Courier Service. With luck, the case would soon be resolved and he'd be back doing something useful instead of babysitting Witch Girl #1.

Pedestrians scurried across the intersection adjacent to the café. All except one lone woman who paused dead center in the crosswalk, juggling a briefcase and a voluminous shoulder bag from which she extracted three cell phones. Without quite knowing why, Luc shoved back his chair and stood, the phone still pressed to his ear.

The pedestrian warning signal guarding the intersection began to blink, indicating the light would soon change. To his concern, the redhead remained oblivious as she sorted through the cell phones she'd unearthed before selecting one that, even from the distance separating them, he could see was a distinctive lavender. A distinctive lavender matching the one in his hand. She swiped the faceplate.

A breathless greeting sounded in his ear. "Hello? Madam?"

Alarm bells clamored with painful intensity. He dropped the cell to the table, took a single step toward the waist-high wrought iron gate separating the outdoor portion of the café from the sidewalk and vaulted over it, careful to land on his good leg. He forced himself to attempt a swift jog, ignoring the red-hot stab of pain that shot from knee to hip. The light changed just then and cars began to move forward.

Get the woman!

The urgent demand roared through him, deafening him to everything else. He remembered his cousin, Nicolò, describing how his wife had been hit by a cab shortly after they'd first met. The driver had changed lanes to avoid a slow-moving vehicle and sped into the intersection, hitting Kiley. Even now, her past remained a blank as a result of the accident, although she and Nicolò were busy building new memories and creating a new life together—which included a baby due sometime in the next few weeks.

Get the woman now!

Luc watched helplessly as history decided to repeat itself. A cab swerved around a delivery truck who'd unexpectedly double parked outside a mom-and-pop market. With a blare of its horn, the cab accelerated directly toward the intersection. Clearly the driver didn't realize the woman was there, probably because he was intent on cursing at the truck driver, while the woman remained oblivious to her danger as she pressed buttons on her cell.

Get the woman now before you lose her forever!

Luc thought he shouted a warning and forced himself into a limping run, cursing a leg that would prevent him from reaching her before the cab. The driver didn't spot the hazard until the very last instant. He slammed on the brakes with an ear-splitting scream of metal and rubber. Luc forced himself to move even faster, praying his leg would hold him, but he knew he'd never be in time.

A split second before the cab hit the woman, it swerved a few precious feet. It was enough. Just enough. Luc snatched her clear and dove toward the safety of the sidewalk. He twisted so he'd absorb most of the impact, landing hard on his bad hip. Raw pain exploded through him.

"Son of a bitch!"

The woman shoved against his chest, surfacing in a tangle of deep auburn curls, lean ivory arms and legs and countless files and papers. Three cell phones rained down around them. A pair of rimless reading glasses dangled from one ear while teal-blue eyes regarded him in open outrage.

"Did you just call me a bitch?"

"Not exactly." Wincing, he grasped the woman around the waist and levered her to one side. Cautiously he sat up. His hip screamed in protest. Aw, hell. Not broken, but not in good shape, either. "Do you always stand in the middle of an intersection daring cars to hit you?" His injury gave the question more of a bite than he intended.

She wrapped herself in indignation while straightening her glasses. One of the fragile bits of wire connecting the two lenses across the bridge of her nose was severely bent, causing the lenses to sit cockeyed on her face.

"I was answering a call from my grandmother." As though the explanation reminded her, she scrambled through the paraphernalia littered around them until she unearthed a lavender cell phone identical to Madam's. "Hello? Madam, are you still there?"

"Téa! Oh, my dear. Are you all right?"

The voice didn't come from the phone, but from a few feet away. Madam and Nonna hurried down the sidewalk toward them. Groaning, Luc cautiously climbed to his feet, then offered Téa a hand. And that's when it hit. A powerful spark, followed by a bone-deep burn shot from her palm to his. It flew through his veins, sinking into him, absorbed on the deepest level.

His internal alarm bells went berserk, clamoring and clashing and shrieking so loudly it destroyed all sensation but one. A desire so strong and powerful he literally shook from the desperate need to snatch this woman into his arms and carry her off. Sweep her away to someplace private where he could put his mark on her. Claim her in every way a man claims a woman.

She stared at him in open shock and he had to assume she'd felt it, as well. Her lips parted, as though begging for his kiss, and her eyes seemed to smolder with blue-green fire. Every scrap of color drained from her face leaving behind a tiny pinprick smattering of freckles dusting her elegant nose. The foam of deep red curls tumbled down her back in bewitching disarray and provided a blazing frame for her upturned face, a face that mirrored every single emotion from bewilderment to disbelief.

She tore her gaze from his and looked at their joined hands. "What . . . ? What was that?" she whispered.

Deep down he knew, though he couldn't quite give it credence. Not yet. Not when it defied logic and understanding. Not when every fiber of his being resisted admitting the possibility of its existence. And yet . . . It was exactly as his grandfather had described. Exactly as his parents had told him. Exactly what his cousins claimed happened to them. And exactly what he'd hoped would never happen to him.

"That was impossible," he answered.

"Téa?" Madam's apprehensive voice cut through the wash of desire. "Téa, I asked if you were all right."

Jerking her hand free of Luc's grasp, she turned to her grandmother. "I'm fine," she assured. "A little shaken and manhandled, but otherwise unhurt."

Luc's brows gathered into a scowl. Manhandled? *Manhandled?* How about snatched from the jaws of death? How about saved by the generosity of a stranger? How about rescued from a metal dragon by a poor battered knight who could have used some

freaking shining armor to protect himself from injury?

Before he could argue the point, pedestrians paused to help gather up Téa's belongings which she carefully organized, tucking everything away into her briefcase and voluminous purse. The desire that had overwhelmed him minutes before eased, at least enough for him to recover her cell phones. One of them was chirping at great volume, urging, "Answer me. Answer me. Answer me, me, *me!*" over and over. Even these had individual slots in her handbag.

By the time she finished, reaction set in. Madam appeared on the verge of tears. Nonna's brow was lined in worry. Only Téa seemed blissfully unconcerned.

Luc, on the other hand, found it difficult to even think straight, other than to resent like hell the events of the past several moments. Pain radiated from every muscle in his body. Between his banged-up knee and hip, Téa's apparent obliviousness to her near-death experience, and that undeniable sizzle of physical attraction when they'd first touched flesh-to-flesh, he was not a happy man. And the fact that Téa was ignoring the significance of each and every part of all the situation, only made it worse.

Luc was a man of action. Someone who took charge. Granted, he had finely tuned instincts. But he backed them with logic and split-second decisiveness that had saved his hide countless times in the past. It had also saved Téa's, though she didn't seem to quite get that fact. Whatever had just happened had done a number on him and stolen control he loathed to relinquish.

Determined to revert to type, he took charge by gathering up the three women and urging them toward the café. After seeing them seated, he went in search of their waiter and ordered a new round of drinks, adding a black ale for himself. If they'd had anything stronger, he'd have chosen that instead, but until he could down a dozen anti-inflammatories chased by a stiff couple of fingers of whiskey, the beer would have to do.

"Thank goodness you were there to rescue Téa from that crazed cab driver," Madam said the minute he returned to the table.

Luc took a seat and fixed Téa with a hard gaze. "Perhaps if your granddaughter wouldn't answer her cell phone in the middle of the intersection, she wouldn't have to worry about being mowed down by crazed cab drivers."

Téa smiled sweetly. "My grandmother tells me you were the one who phoned me. I believe that means this is your fault."

"My fault?" The waiter appeared with their drinks, but froze at Luc's tone, one he used when dressing down some gomer over his latest FUBAR. "How is it my fault you chose to answer your phone in the middle of a busy intersection?"

"If you hadn't called—"

"Which I wouldn't have needed to do if you'd been on time—"

"—I wouldn't have answered my cell in the middle of the intersection."

"—I wouldn't have had to call you. But you're welcome."

He glanced at the waiter and gave an impatient jerk of his head toward the table. Scrambling, the waiter deposited the drinks, scribbled down their orders and made a hasty retreat.

"You're welcome?" Téa repeated.

She blinked, her eyes huge from behind the bent lenses of her reading glasses. As though suddenly aware she had them on, she shoved them into the curls on top of her head. Then her expression blossomed into a wide smile, completely transforming her face. What had been pretty before became stunning.

Heat exploded low in his gut. The urge to carry her off grew stronger, more compelling than before. He snatched up his lager and took a long swallow, praying it would douse the flames. Instead it seemed to make them more intense. All he could think about was finding a way to extract her from this ridiculous meeting and take her off someplace private. To explain in a manner as physically graphic as possible that whatever was happening between them needed to be completed. Several times, if necessary. Whatever it took until the rage of fire and need cooled and he could think rationally again.

"I'm sorry," she said. "Maybe we could start over? Thank you for saving me from being run down. I'm sorry I was late for our lunch meeting. I assure you, it was unavoidable. I don't usually answer my cell phones in the middle of a busy intersection, but it was Madam's and I always take her call, regardless of time and place."

She'd ticked off her points with the speed and precision of a drill sergeant. Where before he'd considered her scattered, now he saw what Nonna meant by her description of Téa de Luca. It would appear she was a woman who existed in organized chaos and operated in focused oblivion.

Luc inclined his head. "Fair enough."

"That said," she continued, "I don't see the point in this meeting." She spared her grandmother a warm smile. "I appreciate your concern, but I don't need a bodyguard."

"Funny," Luc muttered. "Considering what happened just five minutes ago, I'd say that was precisely what you need."

She waved the observation aside. "It could have happened to anyone. Besides, he would have missed me."

It took Luc a split second to find his voice. "Have you lost your mind?"

She patted his arm, then snatched her hand away. Maybe it had something to do with the arc of electricity that flashed between them. Or the throb that shot through the palm of his hand and quite probably her own. With each new touch, whatever existed between them grew stronger, the tendrils binding tighter and more completely. It gave him some measure of satisfaction to see it took her several seconds to recover her poise sufficiently to speak. During the few moments of silence the waiter approached and deposited their luncheon choices. He didn't linger.

"You played the hero quite well and I appreciate your efforts on my behalf," Téa said in a stilted voice. She splashed some oil and vinegar on her salad. "But the cab swerved at the last second."

He leaned in, emphasizing each word with a steak fry. "Which gave me just the extra time and room I needed to keep you from getting clipped by his bumper and turned into roadkill." He popped the fry into his mouth. "He would have hit you if I hadn't pulled you clear."

"Luciano . . ." Nonna murmured.

He glanced first at his grandmother and then at Madam. They both wore identical expressions, a wrenching combination of fear and shock. Not cool, he realized. He'd way overplayed his hand. He pulled back and gathered Madam's hand within his own.

"She's safe and I promise I'll keep her that way."

"Thank you." Tears flooded her dark eyes. "I can't tell you how much this means to me."

"Wait a minute," Téa interrupted. "I haven't agreed to anything."

He shot her a quelling look. Not that she quelled, which amused almost as much as it frustrated. He excelled at quell. Any of the men who served beneath him or currently worked with him could attest to that simple fact. "Not even for your grandmother's peace of mind?" he asked.

It was her turn to be both amused and frustrated. "Oh, very good," she murmured. "Very clever."

"You will agree, won't you, Téa?" Madam's request sounded more like a demand. "It will make all of us feel so much better. Juliann can concentrate on her wedding. Davida can focus on her studies. And Katrina can . . ." She hesitated, clearly at a loss.

"Can continue getting into trouble?" Téa inserted dryly.

"She means well," Madam said with a sigh. "She's just a magnet for disaster."

As though to underscore the comment, Téa's handbag began to chirp again. A youthful, feminine voice demanded, "Answer me. Answer me. Answer me, me, *me!*" Téa smiled blandly. "Speak of the devil."

"So we agree." Luc struggled to be heard over the shrill tones of another ringtone as it added its personalized demand to the first. "I'm your baby—" He cleared his throat. "Your bodyguard for the next six weeks?"

She wanted to argue some more. He suspected the trait was as much a part of her as her red hair. He lifted an eyebrow in Madam's direction and waited, not a bit surprised when Téa caved. "Fine." She lowered her voice so only he could hear. "And don't think I missed that babysitter slip."

He kept his expression unreadable. "I have no idea what you're talking about."

Reaching into the bag, she went through each of her three phones and set them on vibrate. Why she owned so many phones, he had no idea. A subject for another time. Lunch proceeded at a leisurely pace after that and he noticed with some amusement everyone went out of their way to stick to innocuous topics. Schooling himself to patience, he guided the women through the conversation and the meal, before he could finally pick up the check and pay for their lunch. All the while he watched Téa.

Although she chatted with the grandmothers, Luc could tell her thoughts were elsewhere. He could practically see the wheels spinning away, analyzing her problem—*him*—while searching for a satisfactory solution.

"Figured it out, yet?" he asked in an amused undertone.

She stared blankly. "Figured what out?"

"What you're going to do about me."

"Not quite." Then she hesitated and a hint of relief caused her eyes to glitter like gemstones. He didn't need the blazing light bulb flashing over her head to tell him she'd come up with a plan to escape her predicament. "Madam, quick question."

"Yes, dear?"

"How are we compensating Mr. Dante for his time and expertise?" She actually smiled at Madam's small inhalation of alarm. "Bodyguards don't come cheap. And you know we're under serious budgetary constraints for the next six weeks."

"Well, I—"

"Didn't Nonna explain?" Luc offered smoothly. "Consider it your twenty-fifth birthday present from all the Dantes."

"How generous." He could hear the grit through the politeness. "But I couldn't possibly accept such an expensive gift."

He allowed irony to slide through his words. "No, no. Don't thank us. It's our pleasure. Besides, babysitters charge far less than bodyguards. Even if you were to refuse, it wouldn't cost you much at all to hire me." He pushed back his chair and stood. "I'll tell you what. Why don't we continue this meeting in private in order to settle the particulars?"

"Excellent suggestion," she replied crisply and gathered up her briefcase and shoulder bag. "My office?"

Not private enough for what he had in mind. Not nearly private enough. "I have an apartment close by."

"I'm not sure that's such a good idea."

Ignoring her, he gave Nonna and Madam each a kiss. Then draping a powerful arm around Téa's shoulders, he swept her from the restaurant. A cab lingered just outside the door and he bundled her inside, with her protesting all the way. He gave the driver the address to his apartment complex and settled back against the seat.

All the while, Téa bristled with feminine outrage. With her rioting red curls and flashing eyes, she looked like a marmalade cat who'd been rubbed the wrong way. He couldn't quite help taking a certain pleasure in having upset her tidy little world. Considering the ease with which she'd upended his, it seemed only fair.

The cab had barely pulled away from the curb before she started protesting. "I have to get back to work. I don't have time for this. I don't know what sort of game you're playing, Luciano Dante, but I'm not in the mood for it."

"I'm giving our grandmothers what they asked for. If I can spare six weeks out of my life to make sure you reach twenty-five, you can put up with having me around."

"Well, shoot."

He'd clearly gotten her with that one. She took a moment to call the office and inform them of her change in schedule before turning her jumble of cell phones from vibrate to ring, meticulously checking each for messages before stowing them away. Not that she was through arguing. Not this one.

The minute she finished fussing with her phones, she pushed a tumble of curls from her eyes and glared at him. "And another thing, what was that weird zap you gave to me when we first shook hands?"

He gave an "I'm clueless" shrug, hoping it would satisfy. It didn't.

"Don't give me that. I've heard you Dantes have some bizarre touch thing you use on women. It knocks them right off their feet and into your bed." A sudden thought struck and her eyes widened. "Is that what you have planned with me? Are you taking me to your place so you can knock me off my feet and into your bed?"

Chapter Two

"Do you want me to zap you into my bed?" Luc pretended not to notice the cab driver's shocked gaze darting to the rearview mirror.

"No! Of course not."

"Too bad. I'd give it a try even though . . ." He allowed a hint of bewilderment to drift across his face and lied through his teeth. "To be honest, Téa, I have no idea what sort of bizarre touch thing you're talking about."

"Don't give me that." She brushed his denial aside with a graceful sweep of her hand. "Rumors have been flying all over the city about your cousins and how they acquired their wives."

Luc's eyes narrowed. Heaven help him. The woman was like a dog with a bone. He wasn't accustomed to people arguing with him, damn it. Didn't she know she should be intimidated? That when he spoke others leaped to obey? Why the hell wasn't she leaping? "I would have thought you too intelligent to give credence to a bunch of lurid gossip magazines, like *The Snitch.*"

A hint of telltale color underscored the delicate arch of her cheekbones. "It wasn't just the rags. I believe that whole Dante thing was demonstrated on television with Marco's wife."

He dismissed that with a shrug. "Easily explained."

"I'm listening. Explain away," she challenged.

Son of a *bitch.* "A publicity stunt. Marco and Caitlyn are married. Of course she'd recognize her husband, even blindfolded."

He didn't need to see Téa's skeptical expression to know she wasn't buying it. "And that weird electrical shock we experienced? Or do you try that with every woman just to see how she'll react?"

"That's never happened to me," he admitted.

She honed in and Luc began to understand what Nonna had meant about her being focused, though he'd call it borderline obsessive. "What was it? What caused it?"

"Static electricity."

"That was not static electricity."

As far as Luc was concerned, they'd given their driver more than enough entertainment.

"We'll discuss it when we get to my place," he said, hoping to put an end to the conversation. It didn't.

"I'd like to know now," she insisted.

"We'll wait." He inclined his head in the direction of the cabbie and gave her a pointed look. "Until then, tell me what you do for a living."

She turned her gaze toward the front seat, blinked, then smoothly switched gears. "I work for Bling." It was a nickname for Billings, who supplied the Dantes Jewelry empire with their gold and silver needs. "Actually, I sort of own it."

Interesting. "Sort of?" he prompted.

"My grandfather, Daniel Billings, left it to me when he died a few months ago."

"That's your mother's father?" he hazarded a guess.

"No. Mom was married to Danny Billings—Daniel's son—who was killed in a plane wreck when I was a baby. Then, when I turned nine she married my father—my stepfather," Téa clarified. "That's when we were at the lake with Madam. Mom and Dad were on their honeymoon. We de Lucas are a blended family. My sisters are his and I'm hers, but we became theirs and us and ours. All de Lucas in the end with a bit of Billings thrown in for good measure."

The pieces came together. "Got it. Téa seems a rather unusual name for a Billings. Actually it sounds more Italian."

"It comes from a Billings ancestor from way back when. Téadora. It became tradition that the first daughter of the eldest son be given that name."

He tilted his head to one side. "It suits. Or at least, the shortened version does."

"Thanks."

"And you take control of your Billings inheritance in six weeks."

She nodded. "Until then I'm learning the ropes."

A soft bell rang in the back of his head, just the vaguest of alarms. "Who's running the show while you learn the ropes?"

"My second cousin, Conway Billings."

"And if something happens to you before you turn twenty-five?"

She turned her megawatt smile on him again, nearly blowing his circuits offline. "You think my cousin's out to do me in?" she teased.

He took the question seriously. "You'd be amazed what people will do for money. Trust me. I've seen it all."

"Not Connie."

"Connie?"

Téa lifted a shoulder in a careless shrug. "That's what everyone calls Conway. As a bodyguard, you're probably used to looking for trouble, even where it doesn't exist. But that's not the case with me."

She patted his arm in a reassuring manner, the same as she had at the restaurant, then once again whipped back her hand. He found the idea of anyone attempting to reassure him disconcerting. It had always been the other way around. She rubbed the surface of her palm as though it itched or tingled, and he wondered if she even noticed her actions. It took every ounce of self-control not to imitate her gesture. Snatching a quick breath, she glanced out the window.

"Are we almost there?"

"Almost." And it wouldn't be a minute too soon. "Tell me about these accidents you're experiencing."

"I'm not experiencing any accidents." That brilliant smile flashed again. "I'm experiencing a failure to walk and talk at the same time."

It wouldn't be the first time he'd come across a recruit with that problem. He'd get her straightened out soon enough. "You're a klutz."

Her breath escaped in a sigh. "I wish I could deny it. But your assessment is pretty close to the truth. I guess I'm distracted."

"Because of your financial problems?" he hazarded a guess.

"That's part of it. I'm also struggling to learn everything I possibly can before I take over Bling. I never expected to inherit the place, so it hasn't been easy," she confessed. "There's a lot to learn not covered in my business degree at Stanford."

"And you're certain Connie doesn't have a hidden agenda to ensure you don't make it to twenty-five?"

No hesitation. "I'm positive. He's actually planning to start his own business as soon as I'm able to take over the reins. He can't wait to get out from under his responsibilities."

The cab pulled up just then and Luc handed over the fare. After assisting Téa from the car, he led the way up the front steps of the apartment complex to the door. He swept his keycard across the lock and gestured her in. They crossed the foyer and he rang for the elevator. The doors slid open almost immediately and he used his card again to access the top floor. The instant they were enclosed within the suffocating confines of the car, Téa returned to their earlier topic of conversation.

"So now we're alone," she began.

"We are."

Ignoring proper elevator etiquette, she turned to confront him. "Tell me why we keep getting zapped every time we touch. What's going on?"

He watched the digital numbers tick off one by one. After all, someone had to follow proper protocol, especially if it helped him keep his hands to himself. "Magnetic attraction?"

"Not a chance."

"My electric personality?"

She dismissed the suggestion with a delicate snort.

He allowed the silence to consume them while the elevator finished its ascent. The doors slid open directly into the foyer of his suite and she stepped out of the car before freezing. "Good Lord, is all this yours?"

"Yes."

To his relief, her interest in his living accommodations sidelined her questions about The Inferno. "You live here alone?"

"I'm a bit of a hermit." At least, these days he was.

She took her time looking around, examining the Spartan interior, the over-the-top electronics, and the smattering of photos from family gatherings on his walls that offered a few reluctant peeks into his past. She studied each in turn. First the ones of his Dante-filled childhood and those carefree years of raw emotion and puppylike wildness. Then the group shot of his unit revealing his transition to manhood, as evidenced by his uniform and military bearing. It also marked his loss of innocence and rendering of character and spirit until only sheer grit and the drive to survive remained. In that narrow space, life ended or continued based on a confusing combination of fate and experience. And finally, the professional man and the men who'd worked with him, the lone wolf standing ever so slightly apart from the others, who still carried the taint and scars of what had gone before, closed now to the emotional openness of youth. Innocence twisted to cynicism. Joy and hope tempered by reality. Normal, everyday dreams for the future layered beneath caution.

She took it all in, absorbed it without a word, then moved on. And yet, he saw the comprehension in her gaze and realized she understood what so few others had when they'd looked at all those group shots. She'd seen the emotions that existed behind the two-dimensional photos, seen his pain, as well as his determination. She wandered deeper into his sanctuary, forcing him to regard it with fresh eyes. The place would have come across as too austere if not for the warm redwood trim accenting the twenty-five-foot ceilings and the parts of the floor not covered by carpet. She paused in front of the floor-to-ceiling windows and the spectacular view of the bay they afforded with a deeply appreciative expression. Apparently, she approved of the uncluttered look. Somehow that didn't surprise him.

Nor did it surprise him when she gathered herself up and transitioned back to business. "Okay, time for answers," she announced, swiveling to face him. "Before we discuss this bodyguard business, I want to know one thing."

"Funny. So do I."

He approached, impressed that she simply stood and waited for him. Allowed him to reach for her. To take her hands in his while desire exploded around them and through them.

"What is that?" she whispered, dazed.

"That is Dante's Inferno. Which, if I'm not mistaken, means we're both condemned to hell."

Not giving her time to react, he swept her into his arms and kissed her.

Violent heat flashed through Téa, mercurial swift and burning with white-hot need, making her forget her responsibility to her family— something that hadn't happened since she was sixteen. Her reaction to him was identical to when he'd first taken her hand, igniting where their lips melded, the fit sheer perfection. It flashed downward to the pit of her stomach and lower still until the feminine core of her throbbed with the urge to join with this man. It raced through her, tripping over sense and emotion, instinct and logic, turning every part of her inside out and upside down. And still it didn't stop.

The desperation grew so intense that if he stretched her out on the floor of his foyer, she would have allowed him to strip away her clothing and lose himself in her. Just the thought of having him on her, in her, over and around her, joined with her in the most intimate way possible . . . She shuddered.

"Luc . . ." His name escaped on a sigh, became part of the kiss, greedily consumed.

His mouth slipped from hers, following the line of her throat, scalding the sensitive skin as he drifted relentlessly downward. Somehow the buttons of her blouse escaped their holes. The edges of the crisp material separated, giving him access to explore the gentle swells rising above the lacy cups of her bra.

"I don't think I've ever seen skin like yours before. So pale." He trailed a string of kisses along the demarcation line of silken skin and protective lace. "It seems such a cliché to say it's like cream."

She laughed softly. "Not magnolia blossoms?"

He spared her a swift grin, though his eyes remained a shocking molten gold, flaming with a passion unlike anything she'd seen before. "Definitely magnolia blossoms. Only softer."

She didn't know what had gotten into her. This wasn't like her at all. Not the joking. Certainly not the lovemaking. But one touch from Luciano Dante and she tumbled. Her cell phones began to ring and chirp and plead, and with an exclamation of impatience, Luc opened one of the doors leading off the foyer—a coat closet—and shoved her handbag and briefcase inside.

It gave her just enough time to clear her head. "Wait, Luc." Those cell phones were her lifeline. They were a vital link that kept her grounded and connected to her family. Besides, she owed them. She couldn't allow this sort of selfish distraction. "Those calls could be important."

"There's nothing more important than this."

He pulled her close and all coherent thought vanished. How did he manage to do that, when she'd always been so careful with her priorities? Maybe it was because she'd never known real desire before. Not like this. In fact, she'd gone out of her way to avoid it.

Family always came first. Duty and responsibility had been her obsession ever since the death of her parents. She didn't dare let down her guard and surrender to her baser desires. Not since one hideous occasion when she'd done just that and her world had come crashing down around her.

She'd learned her lesson well that night. From then on, taking care of her family became her life. Her obligation. Nothing else topped that one crucial demand. Nothing. At least, nothing until Luciano Dante exploded into her world and—with a single touch, palm against palm—short-circuited every last rational thought but one.

She wanted this man. Needed him. For so many years she'd been in control. The steady leader. The mainstay who looked after her family and protected them. She couldn't and wouldn't indulge her own selfish interest until she'd accomplished that. Once she received her inheritance, she'd be in an even better position to care for her family, instead of constantly scrambling to make ends meet.

But with one shocking touch, Luc took her burden from her. It vanished from thought and awareness, replaced by a passion she'd never experienced, never even knew existed until he'd shown her the stunning possibilities.

His mouth covered hers again, inhaling her, and she simply tumbled. Duty and responsibility floated away, as did reason and intellect. All that remained was a shattering. Intense. Unspeakable. All consuming.

Without breaking the kiss, Luc swept Téa into his arms. She had the sensation of movement from living room to bedroom— a light floating, then a gentle descent, the softest of cushions at her back when they sank into the mattress and a blazing heat that blanketed her. It settled over her, pressing into her, molding hard, powerful angles against the soft, willing give of her body.

She stared up into his face, at the hard, uncompromising features, examining them one by one. He had chiseled cheekbones coupled with a tough, squared jaw. His mouth curved wide and sensuous, bracketed by deep grooves that could convey both humor and displeasure depending on his mood. His hair, cut almost military short, grabbed tight to the darkest shade of ebony and showed a tendency to wave, a tendency he kept under ruthless control. But his eyes dominated his face. He possessed the deep, ancient golden eyes of a predator. Eyes that cut straight through to the soul and lay bare what she most wanted to keep hidden.

He would never be called handsome. Powerful, certainly. Bold. Aggressive. Blatantly masculine. His face had been carved to intimidate, yet contained those elements that—despite lacking prettiness—were wildly appealing to women.

Heaven help her, but he was an impressive male specimen. Tough. A body both strong and muscular, while his touch showed infinite control and tenderness. How was it possible that a man so clearly cut from the cloth of a warrior could also be so gentle?

"What are we doing?" she managed to ask. "What's happening to us?"

"Dante's Inferno."

She shook her head in confusion. "I know it's an inferno. But why is it so intense?"

She caught the smile he couldn't suppress and it dazzled her. "No, that's what it's called. What we're experiencing. Or so the legend claims." He trailed his hand, harshly callused, in a fiery path from throat to breast. She shuddered beneath the dichotomy of rough and soothing. "We call it Dante's Inferno. It happens to the men in our family when they first meet certain women."

She managed a laugh. "How did I get so lucky?"

"I have no idea."

"How long will it last?"

He lowered his head and replaced his hand with his mouth in a leisurely exploration. "I have no idea."

"If we—" She inhaled sharply, shuddering beneath his roving lips and tongue. Her thoughts scattered for an instant before she gathered them up again. "If we make love, will it go away?"

"I hope so." He shook his head with a groan. "Or maybe not. Maybe it'll continue for a while. I wouldn't mind so long as it's not permanent. We could work it out of our systems over the next six weeks."

Relief flooded through her. "But it will go away?"

He reared back, hovering above her like some pagan god. "It better. I'm not like my cousins. They ended up married when it struck. I'm not after the fairy tale, or commitment, or even love. You understand that, don't you?"

"I don't understand any of this," she confessed.

He shook his head as though to clear it. "This isn't permanent." The words were filled with grit and honesty. "This is a temporary affair. It's sex. That's all. If you're expecting a fairy tale ending—"

She allowed a hint of the darkness that had shadowed her over the years to reflect in her gaze. "Don't worry. I don't believe in fairy tales. And I definitely don't believe in happily-ever-after endings."

"But you believe in this." He released the front clasp of her bra and cupped her breasts. Sunshine splashed and rippled across her skin, chasing away the darkness. He traced his thumbs across the sensitive tips, eliciting a soft moan. "You believe in the physical, the same as I do. What we can touch. Desire. Sating that desire. You believe in that, don't you?"

"It wouldn't be hard to make a believer of me," she confessed.

His mouth curved to one side and his eyes glittered like sunrays, threatening to blind her with their intensity. "Trust me. By the time I'm finished, you'll believe."

She found herself laughing, a sound free and lighthearted and utterly alien to her. She bracketed his face with her hands and tugged him down, covering his wonderful mouth with her own. His taste intoxicated her and she rejoiced in the dizzying explosion of pleasure. For long minutes they kissed, slow and sultry. Deep and wet. Learning. Testing. Discovering. But it wasn't enough. Not nearly enough.

Téa tugged at Luc's shirt, struggling to find the buttons and holes and get one through the other. They resisted all efforts and impatient with her own lack of skill, she simply ripped at the edges until buttons pinged all around them. To her delight the edges of his shirt parted and she swept her hands across a broad chest, sharply delineated by gorgeous dips and ridges of toned muscle and sinew.

She'd never felt so free with a man before and she took her time, exploring this one to her heart's content. She rubbed the flat discs of his nipples and bit into his golden flesh, soothing the small mark with her tongue. A soft groan rumbled through his chest, caught within the palms of her hands, and she rejoiced in having provoked the reaction. She'd never wielded so much feminine power. It was a heady sensation.

She took a circuitous route in a southern direction, exploring all the side roads and byways of what she bared, until she hit a roadblock. She made short work of it, her fingers coordinated for a change. The belt parted, the zip of his trousers rasped downward and she slid her hands to the very heart of all that heat and masculinity.

He was hard and swollen, sliding into her hands with greedy urgency. She'd never done this before, either. Never given full rein to her curiosity and her own need to explore. But she couldn't help herself. Not this time. Not with Luc. He didn't stop her or attempt to take charge. Instead he encouraged her with soft, biting kisses and velvety, rough words.

She sensed the effort it took to control himself, could see the iron grip he maintained in order to hold himself back. Instead he devoted himself to stripping away her barriers. Bit by bit her clothes drifted away, her blouse and bra, her skirt and stockings, until all that remained was a scrap of triangular silk guarding her core. She was so caught up in her own exploration she barely noticed.

Until he turned the tables on her.

Just as she familiarized herself with his body, he began to map hers. First her mouth and throat. Then her breasts and abdomen. Degree by degree he turned up the heat, catching her unaware until desire swamped her in great crashing waves, turning her mindless with need. She stared up at him in utter confusion.

"What are you doing?"

The laughter gleamed again. "Can't you tell?"

"We're making love. I . . ." Her eyes fluttered closed and she fought to draw breath, to gather her wits long enough to speak. "I don't remember this part."

"This part?" He spread her thighs and feathered a line of kisses from the curve of her knee to her inner thigh.

"No," she quavered. "Not that part."

Before she could even draw breath, he stripped away her panties. "What about this part?"

And then he kissed her, a kiss more intimate than any she'd ever known before. A climax ripped through her, unexpected and violent and utterly spectacular. The sound that escaped her was part scream and part denial. She'd never . . . ! Not *ever*. Pieces of her lay scattered all over the bed and it was several long minutes before she could gather them up and paste them together well enough to speak again.

"Not that part," she said. "I definitely don't remember that part."

"We'll have to do it again, just to keep your memory refreshed." He fumbled in the drawer beside him. An instant later she heard the distinctive crinkle of foil. "But not right now. Now we have other refreshing to do."

She lay beneath him, stretched in more ways than she could count. Stretched to the edge by a desire that still hadn't been quite sated. Stretched by muscles still quivering and clenching from the aftermath of her climax. Stretched emotionally by a man she'd just met. A man she'd allowed to touch her in ways she'd never before allowed. A man she'd allowed in, or who had forced his way in. She was too overwhelmed to figure out which.

Before she could analyze it further, he came down on top of her. His hands—such tender, powerful hands—slid deep into her hair, anchoring her. Their gazes locked and held, and she felt herself sink into him just as his body sank into hers, mating them together in a perfect fit. She felt herself join with him in ways that were more than just physical. Ways that upended her tidy little world.

And she gave herself to him, totally and unconditionally.

He moved within her and all thought slipped away, replaced by something far more primitive and elemental. A driving need consumed her, an urge to become one. To complete the connection hovering so close. She strained for it. Reached for it. Grasped it eagerly.

Then the strangest thing happened. Téa felt the powerful current from their first meeting complete its circuit. Felt the undeniable melding of man to woman. Knew on some level this moment had changed her on some irrevocable, fundamental level. Part of her shrank from the knowledge, while another part rejoiced.

She wrapped Luc up in a tight embrace, arms and legs entwined. Each thrust came more forcefully, branding her, possessing her. She rode with him while the wildness stirred. It whipped through her, tearing her apart into shiny fragments of desperate desire. She heard him call to her on the whirlwind, centering her. And with each passing moment, each driving movement, they roared toward the center of the storm.

It was an exploding. A shattering. A freefall into the most delicious waves of pleasure she'd ever experienced. Together they soared and plummeted. Rode the wild wind. Together they clung one to the other, joined.

Melded.

Mated.

One.

Téa had no idea how long she lay there, lost in the aftermath of passion. Somewhere along the line every scrap of intelligent thought had fled, leaving behind utter confusion. But it was a delightful confusion, one that left her body glowing with pleasure and her practically purring in satisfaction.

The oddest part was her inability to get her brain back online. Every time she tried, her thoughts would slip and slide in Luc's direction and all she could think about was how he'd taken her. Possessed her. Thrust her into a realm of sensation that had stripped her down to the bare essence of herself and then imprinted what remained with his personal brand. It was as though they'd mixed and mingled to the point where they could never truly separate out their own unique bits and pieces.

"Dear God," Luc rumbled beside her. "I don't think I'll ever be able to move again."

"At least you can talk," she managed to say.

"Okay. I'll talk. You move."

"Can't."

"'Kay. Come here." He wrapped a heavy arm around her waist and scooped her closer. "Aw, hell. It's still there."

She didn't have to ask what. She could feel it. He spooned the hard sweep of his angles against her soft curves. The press of his body cleaving to hers caused the embers to spark to life in renewed need. Every inch of her skin burned with it. Heat blazed along the contact points and she trembled beneath the onslaught.

"Yeah, it's still there." She shuddered in reaction. "Was it supposed to go away?"

"Thought so."

Or did he hope so? The thought flitted in and out of her head as she turned to face him. He opened his eyes, slumberous, yet still hungry. With a soft growl, his mouth came down on hers again, blotting out thought and reason and words. Her arms slid around him just as his slid around her and their legs intertwined once again. They kissed, soft and gentle, then more urgently. An irrepressible need replaced exhaustion, one neither could deny.

Téa wriggled against him. "Luc, please. I want—"

She couldn't even express what she wanted. Just him. More of him. He didn't need the words. He knew. Knew, and responded with a passion that shredded her world into bright glittering starbursts of pleasure. It was as though all the silver and gold from her company somehow melded with the unique fire diamonds from his and encircled them like a ring, creating a bond neither of them were prepared for, nor wanted.

A bond from which they couldn't easily escape.

Chapter Three

Téa awoke with a start and unlike last time, her brain came screaming online, flooding her with frantic messages and warnings. "Oh. My. *God*."

Luc surfaced from beneath her, rumpled and gorgeous and sexier than any man had a right to be. "Is that a please-do-it-again-even-if-it-kills-us version of Oh. My. God? Or have we switched over to what-have-I-done-get-me-the-hell-out-of-here?"

"Um." She carefully untangled male parts from female and put a few precious inches of breathing space between them. It didn't help. Heat and want still pulsated across the breach, threatening to suck her back in. "The get-me-the-hell-out-of-here one."

"Thought so."

With a groan, he levered himself off the bed and limped nude in what she assumed was the direction of the bathroom. Her small gasp stopped him dead in his tracks.

"Oh, Luc. Your hip." Hugging the sheet to her, she crouched in the center of the bed, her gaze riveted on his side. "And your knee! Dear heaven, what did you do?"

His mouth twisted. "I rescued a damsel in distress. Foolish of me, I know."

It took her an instant to understand. "This is *my* fault?" Her misery increased as she took in the huge vibrant bruise that covered his entire hip and edged down his thigh toward his knee. "Why didn't you say something? You must be in pain. Maybe you should see a doctor. Have it X-rayed."

"It's not broken or I wouldn't be walking. I planned to take something for it." A swift, ravening grin came and went. "But I got distracted."

"I'm so sorry. I had no idea you were that badly hurt."

"Trust me, this isn't bad."

She recalled the photos taken of him during his military service and suspected he spoke the unvarnished truth. "And your knee?" She started off the bed, but the change in his expression glued her in place. In an instant he transformed from lover to warrior. To someone she didn't recognize. Someone tough and dangerous, who'd seen and done things she couldn't even imagine.

"Old injury. It has nothing to do with you or what happened earlier."

"But today must have made your knee worse," she said softly.

"It didn't help," he conceded. "My choice, though. And I chose to keep you from becoming cab fodder."

"Thank you." She grimaced as she considered how blasé she'd been about it at lunch. More than blasé. As she recalled, she'd blamed him for the incident. "Seriously, thank you. When I think of how I behaved at lunch—" She broke off with a shake of her head.

"You weren't very grateful."

Ouch. No doubt she deserved that. "I didn't realize. I was distracted." She straightened her shoulders. "Not that that's any excuse. I can't thank you enough for what you did and I'm sorry I made it necessary."

She caught the flash of amusement and realized he was deliberately provoking her as payback for her earlier behavior. And she'd fallen for it.

"No problem," he said. "Next time I'll let the cab have you."

She simply laughed. "No, you won't." If she'd learned nothing else about him in these past few hours, it was that. The words "knight in shining armor" were probably engraved on his soul.

He shook his head with a sigh. "I think it's more a matter of, no, I can't."

He didn't linger, but disappeared through the doorway. The sound of running water confirmed her guess about it being the bathroom. It also gave her an opportunity to escape the bed and gather up her clothing. She winced as she examined the garments. Well, the good news was that most of them could be worn again. Unfortunately, some of the more fragile bits and pieces of silk were beyond use or repair.

Tiptoeing and not quite sure why she bothered, she disappeared into the depths of his apartment, relieved to discover there was a second full bath adjoining his spare bedroom. She took possession of the shower and the various toiletries lined up on the counter. Definitely a woman's touch and she couldn't help but wonder who had left her mark and whether or not she was still in Luc's life. After toweling off, Téa pulled on the salvageable pieces of her clothing and escaped the bathroom. She could hear Luc rummaging through the bureau drawers in his bedroom and paused.

She caught her lower lip between her teeth and briefly debated. She could either sneak out of the apartment like a thief in the night. Or she could face him and deal with the situation. Since there was a real chance they would be stuck together for the next six weeks, addressing what had just happened, and doing it now, seemed the wisest course of action. Plus, she'd never been one to run from a problem. She'd learned long ago to take responsibility for her mistakes. Learned it in the worst possible manner. This one today with Luc had been a huge one.

With a sigh, she made her way to the living room. A quick glance toward the windows revealed the day pausing in those breathless few moments between dusk and true night. Lights from various boats dotted the bay, sweeping straight across the water to Marin County. Off to the left, the Golden Gate Bridge glittered, the suspension cables looking like glowing strands of pearls connecting the city to the northern peninsula. Directly in front of her hovered Alcatraz Island, perched like some mythical land while wisps of fog gathered in a protective mantle about its shores.

Where had the time gone? She shook her head in exasperation. Idiot. She knew full well where it had gone. She'd lost the hours in Luc's bed. No doubt if she went in there and rummaged between the sheets, she'd find all those minutes just sitting there laughing at her.

Luc chose that moment to join her. The fullness of his personality exploded into the room, overwhelming it. "You hungry or should we move straight on to getting drunk and pretending none of this happened?"

She couldn't quite tell if he was serious or not, and suspected a combination of both. She swung around to face him. "I really should go. But before I do, I thought we should discuss things."

"Discuss things," he repeated. He gave her an aggrieved look, one men had patented back in caveman days. Clearly the last thing he wanted was a discussion. "That definitely calls for a drink. You sure you don't want something?"

"No, thank you."

He crossed to a wet bar and pulled out ice and a cut glass tumbler. Tossing in a handful of cubes, causing the crystal to sing, and splashed a healthy finger of whiskey over the cubes. He swirled the liquor in the glass for a moment and then downed it in a single swallow before facing her. She noticed when he pivoted he was careful to plant and twist with his left leg so he wouldn't cause any unnecessary trauma to the injury on his right.

He gestured with his glass, causing the ice cubes to chatter. "Okay. Start discussing. I assume this is the part where you say this can never happen again. That we have to work together for the next six weeks and it would be more professional if we kept things on a business footing. We'll just pretend what happened, didn't. Does that about sum things up?"

He hit too close to home. More than anything she wanted to claim he was wrong. That she was hoping for a torrid affair for the next six weeks and would be quite happy to spend every night in his bed, exploring every possible position and variation of their activities over the past few hours.

"I think I'd like a drink, after all," she announced.

"Smart choice."

"Do you have any wine?"

"Red, white or somewhere in between?"

"Red."

He poured her a glass of something dry and deliciously biting carrying the label from a Sonoma vineyard. She sipped it while considering her options and organizing her points. While he waited, he poured himself a second drink, but didn't down this one. Instead he swirled the combination of liquor and cubes. It took every ounce of effort to yank her gaze from his hand and those long, clever fingers, fingers which had done shocking and delicious things to every part of her body.

She cleared her throat, suddenly aware she'd somehow sipped her way through most of the glass of wine. "Here's the problem," she announced. "The reason we've been forced to work together is because I'm so distracted trying to juggle the pressures of my job and family life. We can't afford to have both of us distracted by this . . ." She lifted an eyebrow. "What did you call it? An inferno?"

"The Inferno," he corrected. "With a capital 'T,' capital 'I' and a whole lot of fire and brimstone in between."

She smiled at the name. Clever. "You said earlier that The Inferno, capital 'T,' capital 'I,' fire and brimstone, etcetera, is a family legend?"

"Yes," he replied, making it clear by tone and attitude he didn't want to discuss it. "Or at least, that's the claim. Never having experienced it before—"

"Until today," she inserted smoothly.

It was like prodding a panther. Those incredible gold eyes narrowed in warning and if he could have snarled, he would have. As it was, he came close. "Hell, Téa. If it makes everything tidier to call a bad case of lust by a more acceptable name like The Inferno, go right ahead. It sure as hell makes it more acceptable to me."

"Lust." She chewed on the word for a moment and decided she didn't care for the flavor. "I thought you said your cousins all married because of The Inferno."

"They did." He threw a lot of emphasis on the word "they." Underscore. Italics. Highlight. Red flashing lights. The works.

She gestured with her glass. "I gather you don't intend to."

"I'm not very good husband material. Too much commitment for my taste." The panther sheathed its claws and he flashed her a smile that practically had her clothing melting off her body. If they could have stripped themselves, they'd be puddled on the floor at her feet. "But I do make a terrific lover."

It was the unvarnished truth, spoken simply and without pretension or bravado. And one she readily conceded. Considering she'd been the most recent recipient, there was no point in denying facts. Unfortunately, there was also no denying the fact she would have loved to have him prove his words all over again. It took a moment, but she managed to pull herself together again, though she did spare a quick downward glance to make certain all her buttons were still safely in their holes.

Reassured, she couldn't resist provoking him one final time. "Just out of curiosity, how do you plan to avoid The Inferno when none of your other relatives have?"

She could see he'd never even considered the question before. She could also see he didn't care for her asking it, or for the fact he didn't have a ready answer. To her amusement, it only took a moment for him to come up with one.

"I'm thirty years old and I've had extensive military training, as well as the skills I picked up running my own security business. We'll either satisfy whatever urges we're experiencing and move on, or . . ." He shrugged. "It's a simple matter of intellect over inclination."

She couldn't decide whether to be amused or insulted. "I believe that brings us back to our main problem. I have to confess, I can't decide which will be more distracting, indulging in an affair with you or trying not to indulge in an affair with you."

"Just out of curiosity. Do I get a vote?"

"Just out of curiosity. Which way would you vote?"

He approached, graceful despite the limp. He took the wine glass from her hand and set it on a nearby table along with his whiskey. Then he caught hold of her and pulled her into his arms.

"I vote to end things right now," he told her. And then he kissed her.

Want blew him apart. Heaven help him, she tasted every bit as delicious as before. Soft and sweet and yet potently female. He liked the way she attacked his mouth, like a succulent piece of fruit she couldn't quite get enough of. And then she would sink into him, savoring him the way he'd seen some women savor a piece of rich, dark chocolate.

Everything about her appealed, from the light, crisp scent of her to the subtle silken curves that had so recently graced his bed, to the wit and intelligence that gave strength to her face and brilliance to the unusual teal shade of her eyes. He almost lost control again, almost swept her up into his arms and carried her back to his bedroom. Maybe he would have if the echo of his last words to her didn't still linger in the air. With a final hungry kiss, he put her from him.

It took her an instant to recover her equilibrium. She stared at him in fuzzy bemusement before snapping back into focus with a soft cry of outrage. "What?" Anger sparked to life, flaming in her gaze and giving her cheeks a rosy bloom. "Why did you kiss me after what you said?"

He shrugged. "I didn't think I'd get the chance again."

He didn't give her an opportunity to reply. Didn't dare. It didn't pay to give women like Téa too much room to fully exercise their vocabulary. Not when they wielded each word with the precision of a marksman and could slice and dice a man with the skill of a master chef.

"I have some associates who can help with our problem. They can take over as your temporary bodyguard."

He couldn't have shocked her more if he'd slapped her. "And us? What about The Inferno?"

"As I mentioned, I have four cousins who described the sort of instant lust we experienced and every last one of them ended up married. That's not going to happen to me. I don't do commitment. And I sure as hell don't do marriage."

"Neither do I," she retorted. "I have more important priorities."

"Excellent. Then we end this before it has a chance to get out of hand. Agreed?"

She opened her mouth to reply, when a muffled voice began to call, "Answer me. Answer me. Answer me, me, *me!*" Her eyes widened in horror and without a word she darted to the foyer and dove into his closet. She emerged a bit more tousled, but with her briefcase and shoulder bag in hand.

She took up residence on his couch and pulled out her cell phones, lining them up with military precision on his coffee table. The ring tone on the first phone—the case a shiny black one covered in neon pink kisses—switched to "Here Comes the Bride."

Téa accepted the call. "Hel— Yes, Jules. Yes, I know. I was in a meeting and couldn't be interrupted." She actually blushed at the lie, then listened for a moment. "Did you check out Divinity for your wedding gown? It won't? Why—" She listened silently for several more seconds. "No, no. I understand. It's just that I arranged for the owner . . . Okay. If it won't work, it won't. I'll get back to you with an alternative. I've got to speak to Vida now. No, she's not more urgent than you. But there's nothing else I can do about your wedding gown until tomorrow. I'm sorry, but that's the best I can do."

She pushed a button with smooth precision and started a new conversation. "Davida, what—" Pause. "Listen up. If you fail that course, you'll be on academic probation. No, I can't get you off again. You'll have to go in and speak to your professor. Well, why did you miss the exam? Oh, for— Yes, that was exasperation you heard in my voice. Recovering from a frat party is not an acceptable excuse for . . . I don't intend to argue the point. If you can't work it out with your professor, you know the consequences." A fraction of a pause this time. "Oh, really? Well, let me spell it out for you. Colleges no longer offer BS degrees in Flirting. If you get kicked out, there's a job waiting for you in the mailroom at Bling. Why, Vida, that's brilliant. I don't know why it didn't occur to me to suggest you speak to your professor and throw yourself on his mercy."

She disconnected the call. It immediately began its "Answer me!" chirp.

"Téa—" Luc began.

She held up a preemptory Wait-A-Minute finger which he would have found amusing if it had been aimed at anyone other than him. "What did you do this time, Kat?" Téa asked the instant she answered the shrill summons. "Again? That's the third time you've been in detention this month. It's also the third time I've had to speak to the principal this month. Listen, I have to go. Madam needs me. I'll see you later tonight and we'll discuss it then."

Luc winced at the way she said "discuss." He didn't envy Kat that particular conversation. Téa hesitated, her hand hovering over the lavender phone that had caused them so much trouble earlier in the day. She caught her lower lip between her teeth, but didn't pick it up.

"Well?" Luc prompted. "I thought you said you took her call anytime, no matter when or where."

"Yes," she confessed. "But I really don't want to answer this time."

Amusement filled him. "Afraid she'll know what you've been up to?"

She fixed her startling blue-green eyes on him and nodded. "She can read minds," Téa answered, perfectly serious. "There's no point in trying to lie to Madam. She knows."

"She won't know."

"Yes, she will. You'll see." The response came out in a "we're doomed" tone of voice. Bracing herself, she picked up the lavender phone and swiped to answer. "Hi, Madam. What's up?" she asked, sounding a shade too casual.

"It's not that she can read minds," Luc offered helpfully. "It's that you don't know how to lie."

She scowled at him over the phone and mouthed, "Shut up," gesturing to give the demand added emphasis. Then she froze, her eyes huge. Guilt stormed across her face like an invading army. "Nothing. No one."

Luc snorted. "Give it up." Crossing to her side, he snatched the phone out of her hand. "Hello, Madam. It's Luc."

There was a brief pause and then Madam said, "Luc? Are you and Téa still together?"

"Just ironing out the final details over dinner."

An almost girlish laugh came across the airwaves. "I'm so relieved you agreed to do this. Nonna was just saying she wouldn't trust anyone else with my granddaughter's welfare, and neither would I."

"Nonna's with you?" So much for palming the job off on his associates. Even if he could get Madam to agree, Nonna would put a swift end to that particular dodge.

"She's right here. The two of us made a day of it. We've been shopping. Visiting. You know . . ." He could almost see her airy wave. "Right now, we're sitting in Primo's garden, enjoying the night air over a glass of wine. Do you want to speak to your grandmother?"

He froze, hoping guilt didn't decide to invade his face now that it was done with Téa's. "No, no. Not necessary."

"It's been hours since lunch. And no one's been able to reach Téa all this time. That's so unlike her. We were starting to worry."

Luc couldn't help himself. It must have been the alcohol that gave the devil access to his tongue while preventing his guardian angel from curbing it. "She insisted on turning off her cell phones while we put our differences to bed," he explained in a bland voice.

Téa made a choking noise.

"Very wise," Madam approved. "I'm just surprised it's taken you so long to settle everything."

"You know your granddaughter," Luc replied smoothly. He fixed Téa with a hot, hungry gaze. "She's very thorough. Likes to examine every inch of whatever you put in front of her and make sure she's intimately familiar with each and every detail."

Téa closed her eyes with a groan and sank back against the couch cushions.

"She is a bit of a perfectionist," Madam conceded.

"I noticed that. And then the minute you think you're finished, she wants to start at the beginning and go over it all again."

"Well the two of you keep at it until you have it just right."

"I'll be sure to tell her you said so."

With that the connection went dead, leaving Téa staring at him with death and dismemberment in her eyes.

"Well?" Nonna prompted. "Luc is still with Téa?"

Madam nodded slowly. "Interesting, yes?"

"Very." Nonna's expression turned crafty and she tapped her finger against her lower lip while she considered the possibilities. "They could not have been discussing the job every minute of all this time, could they?"

"No." Madam drew out the word. "I didn't get that impression."

"So? What do you think they were doing?"

Madam peered carefully around to make certain Primo was out of earshot. She dropped her voice to a whisper. "I think they were having the sex."

Nonna fought back a grin, while struggling to appear appropriately shocked. "Well, we thought we saw signs of The Inferno all those years ago when they first met at the lake as children. Little baby fizzes that suggest what is to come. The same thing happened between Lazzaro and Ariana and look how happy they are together. This simply confirms our suspicions and means we did the right thing when we set this up." A hint of satisfaction crept into her voice.

"You were right," Madam conceded. "But then, you always are."

"Once The Inferno strikes there is nothing they can do but give in to its demands. And maybe, if we are very fortunate, it will keep them too busy to ask uncomfortable questions."

"What questions?"

"You have to admit, that story about Téa needing a bodyguard will not hold up for long," Nonna said. "Luciano will soon discover she is absentminded and when preoccupied prone to walk into walls, but is not in any real danger. We are lucky she had that little accident today or we might never have convinced him to help out."

"Lucky!"

"Now, now. It could not have worked better if we had planned it. No one was hurt and it added credibility to our story." Nonna patted Madam's arm in a reassuring manner. "Luciano is a good boy. Do not worry about your Téa."

"I have always worried about her." Madam's dark eyes glistened with tears. "No one else does. She takes so much on her shoulders. Ever since her parents died. She blames herself, you know."

"Luciano will ease her burden." Nonna's hazel eyes narrowed in thought. "So, step one is complete."

"Step two will be far more difficult," Madam warned.

Nonna lifted a shoulder in a shrug that spoke volumes. "There is always a way to get caught in the act, especially if nature is busy taking its course."

"And once caught?"

Nonna's smile grew cat-swallowing-canary smug. "Why, step three. A wedding, of course."

Luc winced at the expression on Téa's face. She stalked in his direction and snatched the cell phone from his hand. "I can't believe you did that."

"I'm sure she didn't catch the subtext."

Téa lifted an eyebrow. "And if she did?"

Luc felt dull color inch across his face. "Hell."

"You think?" She marched to her handbag and carefully began reorganizing it. "You were right earlier," she said as she arranged.

"Of course I was." He paused a beat. "What was I right about?"

"I also vote to end things right now. Two 'yes' votes makes it unanimous. The motion carries. As of this minute our relationship is strictly business."

He didn't bother commenting, since ending the relationship was what he wanted, as well.

Though why he had a sudden urge to argue the point, he couldn't say. Instead he frowned as the cell phones vanished into her shoulder bag. "Just out of curiosity, why do you have three phones instead of just one?"

"I tried that. There were so many emails and conflicting voicemails and calls getting disconnected or coming in over top of each other, my cell exploded."

His mouth twitched and he found himself relaxing. "Cell phones don't explode."

"Mine did." Her graceful fingers continued sorting and arranging, dancing over her possessions with all the skill of a concert pianist. "After just twenty-four hours the poor thing whimpered like a baby. Then this mushroom shaped cloud erupted out of my purse and the phone melted into a puddle of electronic goo all over everything. It made a terrible mess." She paused, a wistful expression creeping across her face. "A shame really. It was a pretty little thing. I quite liked it."

He folded his arms across his chest and propped his shoulder against the wall. "That's when you bought the individual phones?"

"Oh, no. Then I switched to a smarter smart phone."

"And?"

"It's recovering nicely at the sanitarium. The doctors have high hopes it can be retrained as a dictionary or address book."

Luc grinned, unexpectedly charmed. "And then?"

At long last she appeared satisfied with how she'd packed her shoulder bag and flipped open her briefcase. It was one of those with endless little cubbyholes and slots and zip sections. "Organization is important to me," she said, stating the all-too obvious. "So, I assigned one phone for each need. My three sisters on one, my grandmother on the second and—"

"And?" he prompted again.

She shrugged, burying her head deeper in her briefcase. He suspected it was to avoid looking at him. "And a private line just for me."

"Ah." His focus narrowed, his hunting instincts going on full alert. "Who calls you on that one?"

For a moment, he didn't think she'd respond, wouldn't tell him whether there was someone special in her life. Then she admitted, "Sometimes work." For a split second she appeared intensely vulnerable and self-conscious. "I've been meaning to cancel it. There's really no point in keeping it since I rarely use it."

For some odd reason it took a moment to respond. "Don't," he insisted gruffly. "Don't cancel it."

Now she did look at him, all ruffled and defenseless and clinging gallantly to her dignity. "Why ever not?"

"That one will be our phone."

"Our phone?" She frowned. "We don't need a shared phone. We'll be together often enough you can just tell me whatever you need to in person."

"There may be times over the next six weeks when we're not together and I'll have to get in touch with you." For some reason he found himself speaking gently. "If you'd rather not give me the number, I don't mind sharing with your sisters."

She dismissed the suggestion out of hand. "No, that won't do."

"What about my using Madam's line?"

"Not a chance." She sighed. "No. I guess it'll have to be my private cell."

He searched his pockets until he unearthed his phone. "Give me the number."

Reluctantly she relayed it and he punched it in. "Once I turn twenty-five, I'm going to cancel the service," she warned. She couldn't have made herself any clearer if she'd announced, "In six weeks I'm deleting you from my phone, my work, my life. And my bed."

"Understood," he said, the word ripe with irony.

She stood, and he could tell she was intent on leaving. "Could you call me a cab?"

"Sure. Just as soon as we clarify one thing."

"Which is?"

"This."

He crossed to confront her, his arms closing around her. To his surprise, she didn't attempt to slip from his grasp. Instead her curves settled against his, fitting like a key to a lock. Only this key and this lock were filled with heat and demand. Even more important, this key and lock opened a treasure beyond compare, one he'd never believed existed. One that tempted and seduced.

One he wasn't quite certain he could walk away from in six weeks, though he'd find a way.

"We weren't going to do this again," she protested.

"We weren't going to do this again once we started working together," he corrected. He swung her into his arms. "Our working relationship doesn't begin until tomorrow."

"Your leg!"

"My leg will survive." His lips curved into a wry smile. "It's the rest of me that's questionable."

She teetered on a knife's edge between resistance and capitulation and he waited to see which way she tipped. Then her expression softened into exquisite surrender.

"Well, guess what?" Her arms crept upward and wrapped around his neck. Her lips nuzzled into the hollow at the base of his throat. "Some things may be questionable for you, but I believe I have the answers. Shall we see if I'm right?"

He eyed her with amused appreciation as he carried her to the bedroom. "If you insist."

"Oh, I do insist. In fact, I demand."

"A demand is it?" He deposited her on his bed. "I guess a man has to do what a man has to do," he said with a gusty sigh, and reached for his belt buckle.

Chapter Four

Luc wasn't the least surprised when he woke the next morning to find Téa long gone, no doubt with her briefcase, shoulder bag and cranky cell phones in tow. Some bodyguard he was, allowing his assignment to slip away with such ease.

The apartment felt strangely empty and silent, qualities that until a few hours ago he'd not only prized, but actively sought. He glanced toward the bedside table where he'd stashed his cell phone. He was tempted to try the number she'd given him, but since he'd see her soon at work, there wasn't much point.

He rolled over, planning to get up and shower and make tracks. But something stopped him, the faintest of scents. It sweetened the air next to him, coming from the indentation that was all that remained of Téa. He snagged the pillow and breathed her in.

Her light, crisp perfume saturated his lungs and made him hungry for her. Hungry to repeat the excesses of the night before. But there was another reaction he hadn't anticipated, one that was far worse. His palm throbbed and itched and he found himself rubbing at the sensation just as he'd seen Dante men do their entire lives.

As much as he wanted to deny it, he could feel The Inferno stirring like some great dragon waking from a deep sleep. Flames sparked and crackled, surging through his veins and heating his blood. Not good, he realized in alarm. Not good at all. Somehow, someway, he'd have to return the dragon to its eternal rest. Because if there was one thing he intended to avoid experiencing, it was The Inferno.

He refused to consider that it might be far too late.

Luc arrived at Billings less than an hour later. It was an impressive place, he decided. Thick pearl-gray carpet sucked up all peripheral noise. Not that there was much. The few people he saw spoke in hushed undertones. The furniture was all heavy wood, stained a deep, somber shade of brown. A jungle of plants sprouted from every corner, dense enough to hide a tiger if one wandered in by mistake.

It was all a bit on the stuffy, pretentious side, especially when compared to Dantes. Still, if the purpose of the decor was to give the visitor the impression of wealth and prestige, it succeeded.

The attractive, impeccably tailored receptionist seated behind an intimidating fortress of wood and electronics assured him that not only was Ms. de Luca there, but expecting him. After making a discreet phone call, she examined his identification and presented him with credentials that would allow him to breach the upper echelon of the company's executive offices.

She then escorted him to a bank of elevators and actually pressed the call button for him. He couldn't quite decide if it was the limp that made her so solicitous, or if she just thought men in general had trouble pushing buttons.

Before he could ask, a gleaming elevator accented in mahogany and chrome and playing a soft operatic aria in the background arrived and carried him directly to the executive level where another impeccably tailored receptionist—this one male—escorted him down a heavily forested hallway. He didn't see any tigers lurking in the brush, which disappointed him. But at least this receptionist didn't have to press any buttons for him.

Instead he knocked on a door and opened it before motioning Luc into a corner office. A small break in the march of skyscrapers outside Téa's window allowed for a sliver of sunshine to creep through, along with a splash of grayish-blue water. Luc stepped inside the office and closed the door in the receptionist's face, if only to prove himself capable of that much.

"How nice," he said to Téa, squinting at the sliver of water. "You have a view of the bay."

Téa looked up from her computer screen. For an instant, he saw their last waking moments together reflected in the turbulent blue-green of her eyes. Then she smiled at his jest, robbing him of breath and making his palm throb. Other parts throbbed, as well, but he did his best to ignore those.

"Good morning" was all she had to say to make the throbbing intensify.

"You left." He didn't mean to say that, let alone growl it. For some reason, he couldn't stop himself. "You left without saying goodbye."

"I did."

He didn't quite know what to respond to such a simple and ingenuous admission. He crossed to the window and snatched at his tie, tearing at the knot that threatened to choke him. "Maybe now would be a good time to decide how this bodyguarding stuff is going to work, don't you think?"

"We were supposed to do that last night."

He released a short laugh. "We seemed to spend a lot of last night doing what we weren't supposed to and not doing what we were. How is today going to be any different?"

"We'll start fresh," she said lightly. "See if we can't get it right this time."

He spun to face her. "It felt like we got it right last night."

"Don't."

Images ripped through his mind. Téa splayed across his bed, her glorious hair captured in the final rays of sunlight turning each strand to a blazing, vibrant russet. Téa, her pale skin soaking up the moonlight and glowing with a soft, pearl-white radiance. Those silken limbs twined around him, holding him in the cradle of her hips with surprising strength. The look in her eyes when he joined with her. The sound she made when she climaxed.

His mouth twisted. "Tell me how to stop and I will."

A wistfulness crept into her expression, a hint of the want she'd expressed with such generosity the night before. He could see her swing, light as a summer breeze, between desire and her precious logic.

"Luc." His name escaped on the swing toward desire. "I—"

Before she could complete the thought, a sharp, clear version of "Here Comes the Bride" filled the air. Every scrap of passion vanished as though it had never been. Without another word, she took the call. From what little he caught of the one-sided conversation, Juliana's fiancée was in the military and stationed overseas, which probably explained why so many of the decisions involved Téa. The conversation seemed to go on forever and it wasn't only passion that drained from her face, but energy. She'd just wrapped up that call when Davida rang with an update on her college woes, followed by Madam with a series of financial questions. At least Katrina held off, but maybe someone had locked her in a classroom, preventing her from calling. Or better yet, detention. He could only hope.

Completing the latest conversation, Téa snapped the phone closed and regarded him with an appealing hint of bewilderment. "I'm sorry. What were we discussing?"

Best to let it go. After all, they'd elected to avoid that particular entanglement. "It wasn't important." He tilted his head to one side and decided to probe. He doubted it was germane to the job at hand, but he wouldn't know for certain until he had all the facts. "Is your family always so demanding?" he asked curiously.

She shrugged. "I'm sort of the mother figure."

He asked the next logical question. "What happened to yours?"

"She and my stepfather were killed in a car accident when I was a teenager."

He saw it then, the curtain that whisked across her emotions, hiding them from view. There was a lot more to that simple statement than she let on. Way more. Took one to know one. He also had an incident he kept carefully curtained. Knew how hard she must have practiced to perfect that calm, matter-of-fact tone. How carefully she worded the explanation so it contained the clear statement: Don't go there. I don't want to discuss it.

He let her off the hook. "I gather Madam took you in."

Téa nodded. "She raised us. But it was my responsibility to fill in for our mother."

Interesting. "Who told you that?"

"Who . . . ?" The question knocked her off stride and she blinked at him, a hint of confusion causing her brow to wrinkle. "No one told me. No one had to."

"Uh-huh." He made some swift calculations in his head and came up with . . . way too young. "Just out of curiosity, how old are your sisters?"

"Juliann is twenty-two, Davida is twenty-one, and Katrina is eighteen. She graduates from high school in a couple months. Maybe."

That pretty much confirmed what he suspected. "Which makes you only two years older than Juliann."

"Almost three." This time her response came with a hint of defensiveness.

He throttled back, keeping his comments gentle and understanding. "Right. But even so, it's not quite enough of a gap to make you a mother figure in their eyes." He shot her an easy, confiding sort of grin, one meant to link them in some nebulous way. "I mean, we're both stuck in the same predicament. We're the oldest. We're supposed to set the example for the younger ones. But, my sister, Gia, is six years younger than me and I guarantee she doesn't see me as a father figure. Not even close."

Téa mulled that over, no doubt searching for a flaw in his logic. Eventually she came up with something, though it took her a minute. "Probably because your father's still alive," she said with a hint of triumph. "But when our parents married, they sort of looked at me as if I were—" She broke off with another shrug, her logic running out of steam since her stepfather and mother would have still been alive then, too.

"A mother figure? At nine?" he asked gently.

"Not exactly," she conceded. "But more mature and distant. An aunt or something. I guess it evolved into a mother figure after my parents died."

He tried not to wince. In other words, they made her feel like the odd man out, despite the fact their father eventually adopted her. He thought back to that long-ago summer at the Dante family cabin. How she'd kept herself apart from the rest of them. Now that he thought about it, she'd been different in every possible way from her sisters. In looks—like a flame dancing in the middle of a pile of coal. In attitude—a helpless fawn flitting among a pack of rambunctious panther cubs. In action—an oasis of calm amidst a storm of juvenile turbulence.

"I remember the first time I saw you," he confessed.

"You mean in the intersection?"

He shook his head. "No, I mean the very first time. At the lake when we were kids." He tilted his head to one side, watching the play of emotions chasing across her face, the unexpected vulnerability. "Don't you remember?" he asked softly.

She fiddled with a thick file folder on her desk, flipping it open and then closed again. "Yes," she said after a moment. She lifted eyes gone dark with memories.

"You made me itch even then." The words escaped of their own volition.

She stiffened. Her fingers played across the palm of her hand, though he doubted she even noticed. "Itch?"

He wouldn't admit it might have been the early signs of The Inferno. He wasn't willing to look at it that closely. But something about her had gotten under his skin, even then. "You irritated me."

She didn't press, made a face instead, then accused, "You were a bully. You all were."

It was his turn to shrug. "It wouldn't surprise me. We were probably operating under a pack mentality back then. And you didn't fit in."

She flinched. "No, I didn't."

He leaned across the desk toward her, sweeping a lock of hair off her brow and tucking it behind one ear. His fingers lingered, stroking. "You didn't want to fit in."

"Not then," she agreed, leaning into the caress. "I wasn't used to so much noise and confusion. Before we became de Lucas, it was just me and my mom. We lived a fairly quiet existence except when my Billings grandparents descended. Then it got a bit rocky."

That snagged his attention and his hand fell away. "Why?"

"I don't remember much, but according to Mom, Grandfather Billings was somewhat controlling." She gave a quick half smile, confiding, "Of course he'd have been excruciatingly polite about it. Not like the de Lucas who handle any disagreement at top volume."

Luc grinned. "The Dantes have been known to go at it a time or two, though Nonna will bring us to a fast stop if it continues too long."

"As will Madam. She'll rap her knuckles on the table and if there isn't instant silence—" Téa shuddered.

"She can be intimidating."

"She terrified me during those early years," Téa confessed.

It was a telling comment. "So how did Grandfather Billings take the news that your mother was going to remarry?"

"Not well. He was dead-set against it. In fact, he cut us off when she married Dad." She leaned in closer still and dropped her voice, possibly because they were deep in Billings' territory. Perhaps on some level old man Billings still infused the walls with his essence and she didn't want to chance him overhearing. "It surprised the hell out of me when he named me his successor in the will. Until then I'd planned to get a law degree."

And probably surprised the hell out of her cousin, Conway Billings. Luc decided against saying as much. "You call your stepfather Dad. And you use his name. I assume he adopted you?"

"Yes, when I turned sixteen. Six months later—" She broke off, but he caught the glint of tears in her eyes.

He gathered up her hand. Heat licked across his skin where their palms joined, creating a pleasant sensation. It reassured on some level, as though what had been parted was once again joined and he could relax. "I'm sorry. Losing both of your parents like that must have been rough."

"It would have been far worse if Madam hadn't taken all of us in."

"And now it's time to pay her back for her generosity."

For some reason his observation provoked a smile. "Is that so wrong?"

"You're the one who almost got taken out by a cab because you were so distracted. You tell me."

"It's temporary," she whispered. "As soon as I turn twenty-five—"

"You'll take over the reins of a huge company with limited experience. Your workload will increase dramatically and you'll still have three demanding sisters and a grandmother to worry about."

"You think I should just give it all up?"

"There are options."

"None that will allow me the financial freedom I need." She broke off at the knock on her door and snatched her hand from his. He watched her fight to compose herself before calling out, "Come in."

A man in his mid-forties stuck his head through the opening and gave a patently fake start of surprise. "Oh, you have company. Am I interrupting?"

A smile bloomed on Téa's face and she waved the man in. "You're never interrupting, Connie. Come on in. I'd like to introduce you to Luc Dante. Luc, this is my cousin, Conway Billings."

A man hovering somewhere in those unfortunate inches between medium and short entered the office. Out of sheer habit, Luc made a swift assessment. Conway was dressed in an expensive navy suit with a snowy white shirt, the collar held in place by pretentious gold clips rather than buttons. Matching clips decorated the cuffs of his sleeves. He wore his thinning auburn hair as short as Luc's and kept his ruddy face painfully clean-shaven. He also sported an old-fashioned pocket watch on a real gold chain, no doubt a subtle advertisement of Billings' wares. Gold-rimmed glasses perched on the ball of his stub nose and he kept his shoes polished to a mirror shine. Unlike Téa's creamy complexion, his glowed an uncomfortable shade of red that clashed with his hair.

For some reason, Luc's hackles went up. Maybe it was Conway's pretense of surprise and ridiculous opening question. The door was closed. He had to have heard their voices. Of course he was interrupting. How could he not be? But then, this man ran Billings. At least, for the moment. No doubt his position meant no matter who or what he interrupted, it wasn't an interruption.

Luc also suspected someone had alerted him to the fact that a Dante was in the building talking to Téa. And since Dantes was Billings' biggest client, Cousin Connie wanted to find out what the hell was going on.

Luc stuck out his hand. "A pleasure," he lied.

"Yes, it is," Conway lied right back.

Luc's eyes narrowed. Okay, at least he knew where he stood. He edged his hip onto the corner of Téa's desk, staking his claim, only to ruin the possessive maneuver with a wince of pain. Damn hip. "Nice place you have here," he managed to say.

"Thanks." Pride rippled through the single word. "Billings has been the gold standard ever since my great-uncle established it, two and a half decades ago."

He placed enough emphasis on the words "gold standard" Luc realized it was meant as a play on words. Supplier of gold. Gold standard. Ha-ha. Luc bared his teeth in a grin. "Don't sweat it. Dantes doesn't mind doing business with newcomers like Bling."

Conway stopped laughing. Either Cousin Connie didn't care for the company's nickname, or he didn't appreciate the reminder that Dantes had been around twice as long as Billings.

"Why are you here, Mr. Dante?" he asked bluntly.

"Make it Luc." He waited.

"Luc," Conway repeated through gritted teeth.

"I'm here on behalf of Dantes." He picked up on Téa's incipient protest and turned to her. Catching her hand in his, he gave it a light squeeze. "Just six more weeks, isn't it? We've almost left it too long."

"Left what too long?" Conway asked sharply.

He hadn't missed the touch Luc and Téa had exchanged, an intermingling of fingers that could be taken as a sign of intimacy, and in this case most assuredly was. He regarded the man with the sort of patience one did a child. Good ol' Connie caught the look, interpreted it as just that and bristled in offense.

"Téa takes over Billings then, doesn't she?" Luc didn't wait for confirmation. "As your largest and most important customer, Dantes wants to make certain all our needs will be met before, during and after the transition. So, I plan to work closely with Téa these next few weeks to ensure everything proceeds smoothly."

Téa's eyes narrowed on Luc in warning before she offered her cousin a reassuring smile. "You don't mind, do you, Connie?" she asked.

Conway seized the question with grim determination, using the opportunity to regain control of the situation. "As a matter of fact, I do, Téa," he informed her gravely. "If Dantes wants my assurance that Billings will continue to provide excellent goods and service—"

Luc cut him off without hesitation. "It's not your assurance I'm interested in. You're no longer the one in charge. Your cousin is."

Beside him, Téa stiffened. "Luc," she murmured in protest.

A sweep of heightened color darkened Conway's cheekbones and a protest tumbled out before he could prevent it. "Not for another six weeks, she isn't."

Luc lifted an eyebrow. Interesting. Her cousin sounded a bit possessive for a man who—how had Téa described him? Oh, right. As a man who couldn't wait to get out from under his responsibilities. It might be interesting to find out just what sort of business Conway intended to start up, assuming there actually was one.

Luc shook his head with a mock frown. "Six weeks isn't very long. It might be just enough time for Dantes to satisfy ourselves your gold standard will be upheld after the transition." He lifted an eyebrow. "You don't have any objection to my being here, do you?"

"As a matter of fact—"

"Hey, no problem," Luc interrupted and stood. "If you don't want me around, I'm gone."

"I think that would be best," Conway said with a decisive nod. He appeared more assured now that he'd regained the upper hand. Or at least, thought he had. He smoothed his suit jacket like a bird unruffling its feathers. "I'm sure you understand, Dante. But this is my company—"

"*Our* company," Téa interrupted with a spark of irritation.

Conway started. "Right, right. *Our* company." His tone turned aggrieved. "You must agree, Téa, that it wouldn't be appropriate to have someone looking over our shoulders, as it were."

"Got it." Luc retrieved his cell phone from his pocket and began pressing buttons. "Let me apprise Sev of these latest developments. It's an unfortunate setback, but my cousin is accustomed to those. Very decisive and proactive that cousin of mine."

"Is this really necessary?" Conway demanded.

Luc paused. "What? The phone call or my being here?" He shrugged. "Not that it matters. I assure you both are critical to our continued good relationship."

Téa sliced neatly through the testosterone thickening the air with icy shards of feminine disapproval. "If Conway objects to your being here, Luc, then that's that. Here's what I suggest in order to straighten this out and satisfy all parties involved." She clicked off her suggestions like a general commanding her troops. "Luc, please call Sev and ask if he'll take a meeting. The three of us will go over, sit down with him and see what can be arranged. But make it clear we'll do everything in our power to ensure the transition goes off without a hitch. Connie, since our contract with Dantes is up soon, I suggest we pull together some numbers in order to begin preliminary negotiations on a new one."

Conway stiffened and Luc had the distinct impression he wasn't used to his cousin being quite so assertive. And he sure as hell wasn't accustomed to her issuing instructions to him. "That won't be necessary, Téa," he stated. "I have the contract details well in hand." Frustration ate at his expression before he finally capitulated. "Okay, fine. Mr. Dante, if you must oversee certain aspects of the transition—"

"Luc."

Silence reigned for an entire thirty seconds until Conway bit out, "Luc. If you insist it's necessary to be here—"

"I do."

Conway shot his cousin a smoldering glare. "Since you'll soon be running the show, Téa, you work out all the various details, though I must insist any changes to established routine be run by me beforehand." He hesitated, sparing Luc a suspicious glance. "As for you, Mr.—Luc. I think it only fair you be as forthcoming as possible about your intentions."

"My intentions?"

The question caught Luc off guard and Conway picked up on the fact. He pounced with something akin to triumph. He rocked onto the balls of his feet with a quick bounce and jabbed his index finger toward Luc. "Exactly. Are you really here to ensure a smooth transition, or is this about the renewal of our contract? If you're looking for a better price . . ."

Huh. Luc cocked his head to one side. "Can you offer one?"

"No, I just meant . . ." He eyed the two, his suspicion deepening. "I hope you don't think Téa will offer you a better deal because she's a woman and therefore susceptible to masculine influence."

"Masculine influence," Luc repeated. He didn't need to fake how much the comment offended him. Judging by Téa's outraged inhalation, she took offense, too. "By that I assume you mean sexual influence." He slowly stood, allowing every intimidating inch of his six-feet-three to loom over Billings' five-feet-squat. "Just who the hell do you think I am? And who do you think *Téa* is?"

Conway retreated toward the door. "No! I didn't mean—" A heavy flush stained his cheeks and he made a production of checking his watch. "Since I have an urgent appointment in a few minutes, we'll have to finish this discussion some other time." He fumbled for the door handle behind him. "Téa, you and Luc carry on. I'll be in my office if you need me."

With that, he exited the room with as much dignity as he could muster.

Luc waited until the door banged closed before glancing at Téa. To his relief, he saw amusement glittering in her eyes, replacing her outrage. He edged his hip on the corner of her desk again, managing not to wince this time. "I'm curious," he said. "Could I use sex to persuade you to give Dantes a better deal?"

"Not a chance."

He heaved a disappointed sigh. "Didn't think so, but I had to ask. Sev would have been annoyed if I hadn't at least tried."

"I understand."

"In that case, we better do what Conway ordered."

A delightful confusion spread across her face. "I'm sorry?"

Luc grinned. "Didn't you hear him? He told us to carry on. I suggest we get started." He leaned in, feeling the pull of The Inferno and allowing it to consume him. "He is, after all, the boss."

Her smile turned grim. "Only for six more weeks."

And then she, too, surrendered to the heat.

Chapter Five

The next week passed, at moments feeling as though it were on wings. Other times Téa was certain some sadistic creature had paused the minutes in order for her to fully experience the weight of desire building with each additional day she spent in Luc's company.

It was a desire she couldn't allow. One she didn't have time to explore, not when she faced so many more urgent demands. Mostly it was one she didn't deserve, not after the destruction she'd left in her wake all those years ago— a destruction she could never fully repair even though she'd do her best to mend the few rents within her capability.

Luc kept his word. Except for the single embrace they exchanged after the confrontation with Connie, he hadn't touched her. At least, he didn't touch her the way she longed to be touched. He kept their physical interaction as brief and distant as possible, though she sensed it was as much a struggle for him as for her.

His struggle wasn't implicit in what he said, but she caught his reaction in small and significant ways. The deepening tenor of his voice. The slight hitch in his movement when he reached for her, as though he were deliberately switching gears from intimate to impersonal. A flash of awareness that turned his golden eyes molten with hunger before he deliberately banked the flames.

She didn't find the process any easier. She had an urgent job to accomplish right now, to learn everything she could about her grandfather's company before assuming the reins, while still carving out enough time each day to care for her family's needs and demands. Not to mention the unending phone calls. The last thing she could handle was another disruption. Unfortunately, Luc excelled at disrupting her on every conceivable level, including hiding her phones whenever their constant demands threatened to overwhelm her.

She couldn't say what clued her in the first time, other than the fact she'd enjoyed several hours of blissful silence before noticing her phones were no longer lined up along the edge of her desk. She stared at the empty space for an entire minute, on the verge of panic, before her gaze veered toward Luc and understanding dawned.

"Give them back."

He flipped the page on the journal he read, something dealing with electronic security. "Relax, Téa. Nothing can be that urgent. If it were, they'd call Bling directly."

"That's not the point. You can't just take my cell phones." Her voice rose and she struggled to lower it and even out the shrillness. "They're lifelines to my family. Madam and my sisters depend on me."

He shot her a dangerous look, filled with a hard decisiveness she suspected was a natural part of his personality. Until now he'd never used it on her. "It's vital to trust your team, to rely on them. But it's just as vital to be self-sufficient enough to take care of business if one of those team members is lost."

"In English, please?"

"If you take self-sufficiency away from your sisters, they become less effective on all levels, personal, as well as professional."

"My family isn't some sort of military unit," she protested.

"They'll also never learn to fend for themselves if you wipe their noses every time they sneeze. Your sisters need to learn independent thought and action." His eyes narrowed, disapproval stirring in the deep gold depths. "Unless you want them dependent on you. Is that why you do everything for them? It makes you feel wanted? Needed?"

"No!"

"Are they incompetent? Handicapped in some way?"

"Of course not," she snapped.

"Then why the obsession to micromanage?"

Her mouth tightened and she shook her head, refusing to answer.

He shrugged. "Then, barring emergency, they're perfectly capable of handling their own affairs until after you've finished work for the day. Since I'm in charge of keeping you safe and distraction free, I've made the executive decision to confiscate your phones. I'll return them at five."

"And if there is an emergency?"

"There are enough brain cells between the four of them to call through to the Bling switchboard and alert you to that fact."

She didn't dare admit it came as a tremendous relief to lose the constant barrage of phone calls. And Luc was as good as his word. The moment they stepped foot in her office he took possession of the phones, returning them at five on the dot.

Realizing she'd been staring into space for the past fifteen minutes while he watched on, she forced her attention back to the spreadsheets piled in front of her. "You're not supposed to put your feet on my desk, remember?" she said absently, scanning the numbers.

"I vaguely recall you saying something to that effect."

"And yet, I'm still seeing an impressive pair of size fourteens sitting here in front of me."

"Elevating my feet helps my knee and hip feel better."

She peered at him over the top of her reading glasses. "That's low, even for you."

"Are you calling me a liar?"

"I wouldn't dream of it. I would dream of telling you to move your feet elsewhere while I'm working."

She returned her attention to the numbers. Something didn't add up, but despite her affinity with all things accounting, she couldn't quite figure out what bothered her. She blew out a sigh. Maybe she'd have better luck if the golden-eyed panther lounging nearby didn't constantly distract her, especially when he took great delight in ruffling her tidy little world.

"What's wrong?" he asked.

It didn't surprise her he picked up on her frustration. The man was beyond observant. "I don't know. Nothing."

He dropped his feet to the floor and leaned forward in his chair. "If it were nothing you wouldn't be analyzing the same report for the fifth time this week."

"I'm having focus issues. I'm distracted." She didn't dare admit aloud that a huge part of her distraction sat across from her. "That's one of the reasons you're here, remember? To save me from my own distraction."

His mouth twitched, but he answered seriously enough. "All too well. Part of your problem is you don't get enough sleep."

"I get plenty." She couldn't say for certain, but it was possible the testy note in her voice gave lie to her claim.

"According to Madam you get maybe five hours a night."

She waved that aside. Maybe she'd have been in a better position to argue the point if the numbers weren't doing a bizarre rumba across the page. "It won't be for much longer."

"No, it won't." He caught her hand in his and tugged her to her feet. "Come on."

"What are you doing?" she protested. "I'm working here."

He shot a sardonic glance toward her spreadsheets, then checked his watch. "It's Friday and it's almost four. In my book, that's quitting time."

"Not in mine," she retorted.

"Yeah, well, I'm expected at my grandparents soon for a family celebration. It's Rafe's birthday."

"Oh."

She tugged fruitlessly at her hand before giving it up and leaving it captured within his. Somehow the throb in her palm didn't bother her as much when their hands were interlaced. Instead it calmed her, steadied her, even as it stirred the banked fires of desire kindling between them. She couldn't decide which disturbed her the most, not having the connection created by their touch, or dealing with the urge to tug him into her arms and have her wicked way with him.

She cleared her throat, hoping it would also clear her thoughts. Not that it succeeded. "Well, you go ahead to the party. I have a few more hours to put in here and then, I promise, I'll go straight home." She offered a reassuring smile. "I'll even pay attention to what I'm doing and dive for cover anytime I see a cab."

For the past week he'd escorted her from door-to-door, unwilling to so much as debate the issue. No matter how early she attempted to leave for the office, or how late she stayed, he was always right there to shepherd her to and fro. She had a strong suspicion that Madam played a huge part in alerting him to any unexpected changes in Téa's schedule. After a few days of attempting to circumvent their efforts, she'd given up trying since it proved a ridiculous waste of both time and energy.

"I have a better suggestion," Luc countered. "Why don't you come with me to the party. Then I'll see you home, as usual."

She spared a brief glance toward the stack of accounting reports. They held all the appeal of a root canal. She'd much rather spend the next few hours with Luc. Maybe if he hadn't used the word "party" she'd have considered it. But that word carried negative associations, pushing every last one of her guilt buttons. Duty. Responsibility. Family obligation. They were brands she wore, ones burned into her heart and soul.

Something in her expression must have given her away. "What is it?" he asked sharply. "What's wrong?"

"Nothing." Not that the denial fooled him.

"Bull. You look like someone threatened with a firing squad. Why?"

She lifted her chin and forced herself to regard him with cool composure. "I don't do parties."

He studied her for an endless moment. "How about family dinners?" he asked neutrally. "You have a family, don't you?"

"You know I do," she retorted.

"And your family has dinners, right?"

"Yes, but—"

"And sometimes those dinners are to celebrate a birthday?"

She pushed out a sigh. She could see where this was going. What she couldn't see was a logical way out of it. "It's been known to happen," she admitted.

"That's what this is. A dinner to celebrate my brother's birthday. I'd like you to come with me." And then he turned downright mean and underhanded. "Please, Téa. Come with me," he said softly.

She caved. But then, how could she do anything else? Not only did she want to, but she flat-out couldn't resist the temptation, particularly when it was issued by such a bone-melting masculine package. "Fine. I'll come." She glanced down at her tailored slacks and jacket, the combination in a dignified, somber black. They screamed, "business." "I'm not sure I'm dressed appropriately for a party, though."

"You look gorgeous, as always. Just casual it up."

She blinked at him. "Excuse me?"

"You know how women do." He gestured with his hands. "Undo certain stuff. Fluff other parts."

"Undo and fluff." Maybe if her sisters were here to interpret it would help. Particularly Vida. Téa suspected that her flirty middle sister excelled at the art of undoing and fluffing. "That's man-speak for . . . ?"

"Here. I'll show you."

Before she could stop him, he'd stripped off her jacket and tossed it aside. Then he released the first three buttons of her blouse. While she rebuttoned two of them, he ran his fingers through her hair, releasing the elegant little knot she'd fashioned that morning and sending her hair tumbling down her back in a cascade of exuberant auburn curls.

"Do you mind?" she demanded in exasperation.

"Not at all. All undone and fluffed." He tilted his head to one side. "But there's still something missing."

He took a step back and examined her while she did her best not to feel too self-conscious. "Well?" she asked, squirming just a bit. "What's wrong with me?"

"There's nothing wrong with you. It's just . . ." He snapped his fingers. "Got it." Reaching out, he plucked her reading glasses from the tip of her nose and set them carefully among the papers scattered on her desk. He studied her upturned face and offered a lazy smile filled with blatant male approval. "Much better."

"I need those to read." She wasn't quite sure why she uttered such an inane comment. He just had that effect on her.

"You won't need to read at the party," he answered gravely. "The cake will say Happy Birthday, Rafe."

Her lips quivered in the direction of a smile. "Thank you for letting me know."

"Glad to help."

Téa tidied up her desk and snagged her jacket on the way out of the office. "My phones," she reminded, holding out her hand. For some reason, she felt reluctant to take them when he handed them over. That was a first.

She paused by her assistant's desk on her way out and told him to take off early, before giving in to the pressure of Luc's hand urging her toward the elevators. Five minutes later they were in his car, battling the start of rush hour traffic as they headed toward the Golden Gate Bridge. She used the drive time to deal with the accumulated calls, fighting a headache from the pressure of dealing with her sisters' latest crises. The instant she finished, Luc stole the phones.

"For the next couple hours, you're off duty," he said by way of explanation.

By the time they arrived in Sausalito and climbed the winding roads overlooking the bay, late afternoon was easing toward evening, resting a gentle hand on their surroundings and gilding it with a soft glow. Luc parked the car outside a wooden gate, squeezing in among the other cars piled up there. The gate led to a lush backyard, with rambling flowerbeds rioting in color and fragrance. Carefully pruned black acacia and bay trees shaded portions of the large, fenced oasis while a mush oak spread its protective arms over a wrought iron table and chairs. The dining area offered the perfect place for an outdoor lunch or supper, with its glorious view of the bay, Angel Island, and Belvedere. Currently, nearly a dozen people gathered there, all of whom were talking and laughing at full volume, some in English and some in Italian.

Luc didn't approach immediately, but pulled Téa close and murmured in her ear. "Hang on a minute. You met the original Dante clan when we were children, but I don't expect you can put names and faces together after all these years."

"Not a chance," she admitted.

"I'll give you a quick rundown. First up are the cousins." He indicated one of the men sitting near the table. He was a couple years older than Luc and bore a striking similarity in appearance. "Have you taken any meetings with Sev, yet?"

"Connie's covering that for now." She couldn't explain why she felt so reluctant to admit as much. Nor why she hastened to add, "I expect I'll have the chance to sit down with Sev when we finalize a new contract."

"Well, you can at least press the flesh tonight." He indicated two particularly gorgeous men with dark brown hair and Nonna's hazel eyes. "Those are the twins, Marco and Lazz. And their youngest brother, Nicolò, is sitting in the grass with his wife, Kiley."

Next Luc indicated a heavily pregnant blonde snuggled in Sev's arms. "That's his wife, Francesca. She and Kiley are due . . ." He made a production of checking his watch.

Téa lifted an eyebrow. "That soon?"

"Oh, yeah." He continued pointing out relatives. "Marco's wife, Caitlyn, is talking to Lazz's wife, Ariana. And my sister, Gia, is the one pouring the wine. Come on and I'll introduce you to everyone." He offered a swift grin. "Take a deep breath—"

"And dive right in?"

"The water's nice and warm."

Téa expected to feel like an outsider, but the Dantes soon proved her wrong. Perhaps it was because the family was so large and sprawling or because there were so many diverse personalities, but they instantly made her feel like one of them.

Gia, the most outgoing and vibrant of the bunch, gave her a quick hug and pressed a glass of wine into her hand. And while the men discussed all things sports related, the women talked at length about the additions that were soon to grace the family.

"So far Nonna is batting a thousand." Ariana dropped the comment into a lull in the conversation, speaking with the lightest of Italian accents.

"What do you mean?" Kiley asked.

"Well, she said you both would have boys and that's what the ultrasound shows, yes?"

"True," Francesca admitted, rubbing the taut mound of her belly. "But then, she also said you'd have the only girl out of all these Dantes sprawled around here."

"Also true," Ariana said.

It took a split second for comprehension to sweep through the family. The instant it did, a half dozen different voices exploded in everything from cheers of excitement to a rapid-fire peppering of questions.

"When are you due?"

"Is it really a girl?"

"Why didn't you tell us sooner?"

Lazz held up his hands with a laugh. "She's due in a bit under six months. We wanted to keep it to ourselves for a while without you lot driving us crazy. And yes, the ultrasound confirmed today that it's a girl. A bit early for them to know, or so I've been told, but apparently the baby was positioned just right for the doctor to make the determination."

Téa and Luc enjoyed the added celebratory mood of the family while they finished their drinks. Then he urged her to her feet. "Let's go inside and say hello to Primo and Nonna."

They found Primo supervising the kitchen, a bottle of homemade beer at his elbow. The room was enormous, with huge bluish-gray flagstones decorating the rustic kitchen floor. Overhead, rough-hewn redwood beams stretched across the twelve-foot plaster ceiling. A long, broad table, one designed for the largest of families, took up one end of the room, while appliances suitable for a gourmet kitchen filled the other. Several more Dantes were busy carrying out Primo's orders as they put the finishing touches on the various dishes they were preparing for dinner. To Téa's surprise all of them were male.

"I'm beginning to like your family," she told Luc in an undertone.

He grinned, quick on the uptake. "Because the men cook?"

"Darn right. Makes a nice change. Of course, there aren't any men in my family, only women, so we get stuck with all the chores."

"Cooking and gardening are my grandfather's two favorite pastimes. Wait until you try his *pollo al Marsala con peperoni rossi.*" Luc closed his eyes in ecstasy. "There are chefs from all over the world who'd give their eyeteeth for the recipe."

"Chicken Marsala with red peppers?" she hazarded a guess. "My Italian isn't that great, much to Madam's displeasure." She slanted him a quick, teasing grin. "Except when it comes to food."

"We'll have to see what we can do to change that."

The expression in his eyes made her feel as though she were free-falling at fifteen thousand feet without a parachute. Heat exploded deep in her belly and spread outward in waves of lapping fire. All thought vanished, except for one indisputable fact. This was her man. She didn't know how it had happened or why, but he belonged to her every bit as much as she belonged to him. Even as the crazy thought took hold, she struggled to dismiss it. It was wrong to put her personal desires first. But some thoughts couldn't be so easily dismissed.

Primo paused in the middle of barking an order to greet them. "So," he said, the flavor of his Tuscany homeland filling his words with a lyrical warmth. "This is the one, yes?"

Téa wasn't certain who appeared more alarmed, her or Luc. She'd always considered herself in control of her emotions and able to keep them well hidden from curious eyes. She hoped she'd nailed the ability, considering she'd been practicing since the tender age of sixteen. But, with Primo . . . It was as though he looked into her heart and laid it bare. And she didn't like it one bit. Deciding to take control of the situation, she stuck out her hand.

"How do you do, Mr. Dante. I'm Téa de Luca. Luc and I are working together. *Temporarily.*" Though who that final word was aimed at—Luc, his grandfather, or herself—she couldn't quite say.

"Mr. Dante?" he repeated with an offended click of his tongue. He wrapped her up in a powerful hug filled with the distinctive scent of a fragrant cigar and a variety of the spices he'd used in the preparation of their dinner. "I am Primo, you understand?"

"Primo," she said, accepting the enthusiastic kisses he planted on each of her cheeks. "It's a pleasure to meet you."

He drew back in mock offense. "We met when you were a little girl. You do not remember me? With most people I make a big impression."

She fought to control her amusement, not wanting to offend. "I'm sorry. I remember the cabin and the lake, but not too much else."

Primo lifted a sooty eyebrow and fixed her with ancient gold eyes that were identical to Luc's. "Well, no matter. I remember you. You were a pale, shy thing, overwhelmed by so many people. All bright red hair and white, skinny arms and legs." He touched the tip of her nose. "Always had this stuck in a book, yes?"

"That was me," she admitted with a laugh.

Primo turned and slapped the shoulder of one of the men behind him with a hand heavy enough to knock him to the floor. Maybe it would have if he hadn't possessed a powerful Dante build. "This is Luc's *babbo,* Alessandro."

Luc's father, Téa realized. At least, the Tuscany version of the word. The weight of Dante genes rested heavily on the three generations of men. "It's a pleasure."

"I'm stirring or I'd come over and say hello." Alessandro tossed a friendly smile over his shoulder. "Hello, anyway."

"You stir, I say hello," Primo instructed. He pointed to the next one in line. "This is Rafe. He is one of the pretty Dantes. We only have two, thank the good Lord above for that small blessing. One is a girl, my precious Gianna, which is as it should be. We keep the other despite his being as pretty as the girl. If he did not have a brain, I would have drowned him as a child."

"I believe you tried that, Primo," Rafe offered, "and discovered I could swim like a fish."

"I should have tried harder." Primo whacked his next helper. "And this good-for-nothing is Draco. I am not certain what use he is."

"I'm the charming one."

"Marco is the charming one. You are *l'stigatore*. The troublemaker."

Draco shrugged, not bothered by the accusation. "That, too."

"That, alone," Primo corrected before addressing Luc once again. *"Cucciolo mio,* go find Nonna and Elia and introduce Téa. Maybe she will remember your *mammina* better than she remembers me." He leaned toward Téa, confiding, "I do not let them in the kitchen until it is time to eat."

"Sounds perfect to me," Téa said with sincere appreciation.

Primo grinned. "I like you. You come back when all is ready and sit next to me."

The offer touched her. "Thank you. I look forward to it."

The night seemed to fly by after that. As ordered, Téa took the seat of honor beside Primo and surprised herself by eating every morsel put in front of her. She also discovered Luc was right. Primo's Marsala was sheer ambrosia. Dinner took hours, the process a raucous occasion filled with genuine family affection and laughter.

The cake did indeed say, Happy Birthday, Rafe, and after it was consumed, the presents opened, and the dishes washed, the women swept Téa off to enjoy coffee and talk babies some more. She threw a panicked glance over her shoulder in Luc's direction, but he just chuckled at her dismay. The last view she had of him was his glorious grin before it dissolved into a sudden frown. It took her a moment to understand why. But then she saw it. He was staring down at his hands. Staring at the unconscious massage of left thumb against right palm. Staring as though his hands didn't quite belong to his own body.

Staring at the undeniable proof The Inferno had claimed another victim.

"*So, it has finally struck,*" Primo said the instant the women left.

Luc glanced up in confusion while his brother, Rafe, looked on with an amused expression on his too-handsome face. "Excuse me?"

"The Inferno." His grandfather gestured toward his grandson's hands. "Do not bother denying it, Luciano. The signs are all there."

"What this?" He deliberately gave his palm a final scratch and forced a laugh. "Just an itch."

Primo snorted. "What you feel is a fifty-year itch, boy. Longer if you are very lucky."

"Téa de Luca is an assignment, nothing more."

Primo rolled his eyes heavenward. "Why are they always so stubborn? So reluctant to believe the truth even when it strikes as hard and dazzling as a lightning bolt?"

He crossed to one of the cabinets and pulled out a canister that read, Dried Manroot. Popping the lid, he extracted a cigar while Luc struggled to suppress a snort of laughter,

Day Leclaire

thoroughly enjoying his grandfather's sense of the absurd.

"Nonna will have a fit if she sees you with that," Rafe warned, his jade-green eyes gleaming in shared amusement.

"Then we will make certain she does not see." He took a moment to prep the cigar, then light it. "Luciano, you have witnessed The Inferno every day of your life. With my beloved Nonna. With your parents. One by one, with each of your cousins." He lifted a snowy eyebrow. "Did you believe yourself immune?"

Luc set his jaw at a stubborn angle. "Yes."

Primo blew a ring of smoke skyward and shrugged. "You were wrong."

"I'm not interested in settling down," Luc protested. "I'm sure as hell not interested in marriage and children."

"Because of what happened?" his grandfather asked shrewdly.

There was no point in denying the truth. "Yes."

Luc shied from the memories, knowing if he didn't build a strong enough bulwark, they'd consume him. One key lesson had come from the incident, an undeniable fact he'd learned about himself. He never wanted to give so much of himself to another person he couldn't live without her. To trust to that extent. To risk so much. Rafe had warned him when his own marriage had ended in disaster. But the accident that had ruined Luc's knee had brought the fact home in spades.

Primo stabbed his cigar in Luc's direction. "The Inferno is not something you can simply turn off. It has happened and you will have to deal with it. You can do as your uncle did, God rest my Dominic's soul." He crossed himself, grief still haunting his black eyes. "Like Dominic, you can turn from it and destroy your life. Or you can follow your parents' excellent example. You can embrace it and discover a happiness unlike anything you could imagine."

"And when it ends?" Luc demanded.

Primo regarded him in bewilderment. "What is this ending? Who says it must end?"

"All things end," Luc insisted in a hard voice. "Love is a gamble, the ultimate gamble. When it ends, you don't just lose. It can destroy you. I've seen it happen. That's why I'll never give into it, why I only bet when I know I can win."

Understanding dawned in his grandfather's face and an uncomfortable compassion settled into the deep lines bracketing his mouth. "You speak of the accident, yes? That unfortunate family?" He didn't wait for a response. "Death is part of life, Luciano, just as love is. No one can control it. You witnessed that during your military service. Everything in life is a risk. But you can't win unless you play. Take the love while you have the chance. Worrying about the other does you no good."

Nonna's voice drifted in from the backyard, warning of her approach. Without hesitation, Primo snatched his cigar from between his teeth and shoved it into Luc's hand. By the time his wife entered the kitchen, he was across the room with a virtuous expression pinned to his face.

Nonna's hazel eyes landed on Luc before arrowing toward Primo. "You know what the doctor said about smoking. No more cigars."

"Do you see a cigar in my hand, old woman?"

"Do you think me a fool, old man?" After nearly sixty years of marriage, her imitation of her husband was uncanny.

Primo held his hands out. *"Che cosa?* I have no idea what you are talking about."

"You look as innocent as a wolf with a lamb between its teeth, Primo Dante. My Luciano does not smoke." Nonna planted her hands on her hips. "You think I do not know the meaning of dried manroot? I know all about that canister in your spice cabinet."

"Dried cucumber," he protested. "Just a bit of seasoning."

"Hah! A joke at my expense, is what it is. Only the joke is on you when I tell all our friends that Primo Dante keeps his dried manroot in a jar in our kitchen cabinet!"

"You would not dare!" He thumped his chest. "I am your husband and I am telling you—"

She lifted an eyebrow.

Primo cleared his throat. "And I am telling you that as of tonight there will be no dried manroot in my spice cabinet."

She nodded in satisfaction. "I thought that might be what you wanted to tell me."

Chapter Six

The evening didn't end as well as it began.

Téa expected Luc to join her after he'd finished his conversation with Primo. But instead, Sev Dante, the head of Dantes, the family's international jewelry empire, slipped into the seat next to hers. She offered him a smile, one he didn't return.

Her smile faded. "Is something wrong?"

He frowned, adding to her concern, and kept his voice low, so their conversation didn't carry to the other Dantes sprawled around them. "I know a birthday party isn't the appropriate venue for this discussion, but Francesca insisted I speak to you," he began on an ominous note. "She's usually right about these things."

"What things?" Téa asked warily.

"Business matters."

She stiffened. This couldn't be good, not when it involved so much frowning. "Business matters. As in Billings' contract with Dantes?" At his nod of confirmation, she said, "I thought Connie was handling that."

He studied her with a golden gaze remarkably similar to Luc's, if perhaps a shade tawnier. "Let's just say your cousin hasn't been very responsive to the concerns I've raised. So if he's representing you in this matter, he's not doing a very good job of it." He hesitated, then asked, "You'll be in charge of Bling soon, won't you?"

"Five more weeks," she acknowledged.

"Then you should know there's a strong possibility that Dantes won't re-up our contract."

She fought to keep all emotion from her expression while she figured out how to deal with the unexpected—and alarming— information. All the while, a thread of panic wormed through her. If they lost the Dantes account, the company would be in serious jeopardy. Other accounts might follow suit and her inheritance would go from impressive to nonexistent.

And that meant she'd fail her family.

"Can you tell me why you've changed your mind about doing business with Billings?" she asked with impressive calm.

"It's a quality issue. Yours has gone down while your prices have skyrocketed. Conway says it's at your insistence. We've had another company approach us offering far better prices and top-notch quality."

Téa straightened in her chair. She carefully returned her cup and saucer to the wrought iron table and swiveled to confront Sev directly. "No one offers better quality than Billings."

"Once upon a time that would be true," he acknowledged. "But not any longer."

She searched desperately for a solution. "What if I can guarantee both? Would you re-evaluate your decision?"

"Your guarantee doesn't hold a lot of weight considering the quality of the merchandise we've been receiving." He hesitated, then nodded. "But since our two companies have always enjoyed such a stellar relationship, I'll give you a couple of weeks to get to the bottom of the problem."

"Thank you. I'll look into the matter and call you Monday, at the latest."

Sev inclined his head. "One last thing."

He shot a look over her shoulder. Téa didn't need to follow his glance to know that Luc was approaching. She could feel him. Feel him as though he were a rising tide and she the waiting shoreline.

"Yes?" she prompted.

"Your association with Luc won't influence my decision," Sev warned quietly. And with that, he stood and returned to his wife.

Luc shot a glance in Téa's direction and grimaced. Ever since they'd left his grandparents' house, she hadn't said more than a half dozen words, but had wrapped herself in silent gloom. Streetlights flickered over her, giving a harsh highlight to the tension scoring her face.

"Okay, what happened?" he demanded.

She was so lost in thought he couldn't be certain she'd heard him until her voice slipped out, soft as the night. "Nothing happened. It was a lovely evening." Then as an afterthought, she added politely, "Thank you for inviting me."

"You're welcome. Now what the hell is wrong? And don't tell me nothing. Something happened."

She swiveled slightly to face him. "Maybe I will tell you what happened. I realized where I've been going wrong all this time. I realized my distraction is causing me endless problems and that it has to stop."

That was good, right? "That's good, right?" So why had his alarm bells kicked in?

"It's excellent." She managed a wobbly smile that didn't convince either of them. "In fact, it's so excellent I'm not going to need your services any longer."

His hands tightened on the steering wheel. "Good try, but not a chance in hell."

"Madam hired you because I was distracted," she reminded him. "I'm not distracted, anymore. I've never seen the situation more clearly."

He wished he could accuse her of having consumed too much of the wine that had flowed like water that evening. But he'd be surprised if she'd sampled more than the single glass she'd been handed when they first arrived. He didn't know who had said what this evening, but he wasn't about to let her off the hook just because a single night with his relatives had—*hallelujah*—given her 20/20 vision.

He used the only lever he possessed. "I'm your birthday present, remember?" Was it his fault if the words came out gravel-rough? "You can't unwrap or return me until you turn twenty-five."

She didn't so much as crack a smile. "You can insist on babysitting me for the next five weeks. It's not like I'm strong enough to turf you out, not with Madam and Nonna in your corner. But I don't need your assistance any longer. I'm more focused than I've ever been in my life."

He shot her a curious look before returning his attention to the road. "Uh-huh. And what brought that on?"

"Tonight helped me figure out my priorities."

That was good, right? "That's good, right?" he repeated.

"That's excellent," she confirmed again. "From now on, I follow the Dantes' stellar example. I put family first. I have to if I'm going to protect them."

"Uh . . . Great?" Damn it.

"Yes, great." Her face settled into a grim, determined expression that set his alarm bells ringing to the max. "Because it means I put all my time and focus into taking over Billings." That was not good. Not even a little. "All your time and attention?"

"Twenty-four/seven," she confirmed.

"That's what you learned from someone at Primo's tonight?"

"That's what I learned."

"Got it."

He didn't know which Dante was gonna die, but one of them was going down for whatever bug they'd stuck in Téa's ear. He'd been where she was, devoting his life to a cause. And it had just about killed him. Literally. It was bad enough when she was striving for some sort of balance between work and family and the teeny-tiny sliver of a piece he'd managed to coax out of her for play. Now it would only get worse. And someone would pay. Someone always paid the price for that sort of dedication.

He just didn't want it to be Téa.

First thing Monday, frustrated as a tiger with its tail in a knot, Luc watched Téa take the first step in her campaign. She marched into Conway Billings' office—a huge, palatial room with a prime view of the city—and slammed the door in Luc's face. The conversation between cousins went on at some length before she returned. She didn't even glance at him, though one look at her burning eyes and taut jaw warned her conversation with "Cuz" didn't go well. She made a beeline for her own office and the spreadsheets she'd left there on Friday. She spent three straight hours poring over them, her expression more severe than he'd ever seen it.

At one point, she sent him from the room while she made a series of phone calls. Something was definitely up. He waited outside her office, glancing in the general direction of Conway's and snagged his cell from his back pocket. He scrolled through the names until he hit on the one he wanted and placed the call.

"Juice? It's Luc. I need you to run a full background check on someone for me."

"What happened to hello?" Dantes' head of security and his former business associate complained in a rumbling bass voice. "You used to at least soften me up with a, 'how's it going?' before you started in. I feel so used when you insist we just get straight to it."

Luc felt his mouth relax into a grin. "Then you shouldn't let strangers pick you up in bars."

Juice sighed. "True enough. What can I get you?"

Luc gave him the details. "Rush it, will you?"

"That's not what they usually say."

"Yeah, but at least I'll still respect you in the morning. And I promise I'll call you soon. Honey."

Juice snorted. "Stuff it," he said before the line went dead.

Luc turned to find Téa standing there, arms folded across her chest, her vivid teal-blue eyes glaring through the sparkling lenses of her reading glasses. "If you're quite finished?"

"All done," he confirmed cheerfully.

"I'm going on a business trip, which means you get the next couple of days off."

He waited a beat. "No, I believe it means I'm going on a business trip, too," he corrected.

She sliced a hand through the air. "Unnecessary and out of the question. It's a matter of confidentiality."

"I'm all about confidentiality."

"Not this time. I need to do this on my own. Connie insists and I'm forced to agree."

"Oh, well. If Connie insists." He backed her into the office, slammed the door closed and shoved his nose against hers. Awareness shimmered through him, an awareness he did his level best to ignore. "Then I'm absolutely going."

Her eyes narrowed and he could practically see the gears spinning. Then she drew back and offered a wide, insincere smile. "Fine," she said with a careless shrug. "You can come, too."

He didn't need any alarm bells to know she'd given in way too easily. Plus, there was the small matter of her utter and total inability to lie. "When and where?"

"Wednesday morning, first thing."

"Got it." He lifted an eyebrow. "I'll pick you up at the usual time tomorrow?"

Her smile returned, sunny with insincerity. "Of course."

Of course.

Luc was right.

He'd suspected Téa planned to sneak out bright and early Tuesday morning and she didn't disappoint him. He stood wrapped in early morning dew and shadows, and rested his hip against the brick wall that guarded the de Luca family row house. Somehow, the Italianate Victorian suited them, with its trademark gingerbread accents, top-heavy cornices and long, hooded windows. The garage door opened and Téa backed her car carefully out before the electronic mechanism engaged and slid the door closed again. He shifted until he stood directly in her path.

The instant she caught sight of him in her rearview mirror, her brakes squealed and the car bounced to a stop. After turning off the ignition, Téa erupted from the car. She made a beeline toward him, the decisive click of her heels bouncing off the concrete driveway.

Somebody didn't look happy to see him. He was crushed.

"I. Should. Have. *Known*." She bit off each word as if they were chewed nails.

"Yeah, you should have." He held out his hand. "Keys."

"You're not coming."

He didn't bother arguing. He let his expression say it all.

She stewed for an entire sixty seconds before relenting. "If you must come, then I insist on driving."

He simply stood there, as immobile as a rock, hand outstretched.

"I'm sure there's a rule somewhere that says that bodyguards ride shotgun." When he still didn't budge, she slapped the keys in his hand. "Fine. I'll navigate."

"Excellent decision."

"It's not like I had a choice," she grumbled.

"Sure you did."

She lifted an eyebrow. "I could have canceled the trip?"

His mouth kicked up at the corners. "You got it."

He keyed the fob and popped the trunk. Picking up his duffel bag from where he'd stashed it on the sidewalk, he stowed it alongside Téa's case. By the time he finished Téa was already in the car, her nose buried in a map book.

Luc eased his tall frame behind the wheel and adjusted the seat to accommodate his long legs and cause his knee the least amount of strain. Twitched the mirrors. Did a quick check of the various controls. The engine turned over with a soft purr that spoke of a well-maintained vehicle. Knowing Téa he was willing to bet she rolled in for servicing at the exact same instant the odometer rolled past each three thousand miles.

He didn't really need directions for getting out of the city, but if telling him where to go helped Téa come to terms with his crashing her business trip, he'd put up with it.

"How did you know?" she finally asked once they cleared the city.

"I know you." He shot her a speaking look. "Plus, you have to be the world's worst liar. Probably comes from lack of practice."

"You say that like it's a bad thing."

"It can be. I'm willing to bet every one of your sisters excels at the art."

She mulled that over before conceding the truth of it. "There are a lot of arts my sisters excel at that I don't."

No doubt it was part of the reason she'd never quite fit in. "And I thank God for it." He gave her a moment to digest his comment, then asked, "Care to tell me where we're going and why?"

"Connie asked me to visit some of our smaller accounts along the coast between San Francisco and L.A., so we can all get to know each other before I take over."

"Uh . . . I hate to tell you this, but Sacramento isn't between San Francisco and L.A. And that's the direction you have us headed."

"That's because I'm not going to visit those accounts."

"I'm shocked." And he was. "You're flouting Conway's authority?"

"Why, yes. I believe I am. I've always wanted to learn how to flout." Her chin took on a stubborn slant. "And today's the day."

He couldn't help himself. He chuckled. "Where are we going, instead?"

"To talk to the former manager of our manufacturing plant." She pulled out a piece of paper from her shoulder bag and checked the directions against the map book. "He retired to some small town called Polk about the time I started at Bling. It's located in the Sierra Nevada Mountains."

"Never heard of the place. Why do you want to talk to him?"

She hesitated for a telling moment. "To find out why he retired and what changes have been instituted since he left."

He considered how she'd obsessed over the accounting spreadsheets, obviously troubled by something she'd found there. It wasn't difficult to put two and two together and come up with Cousin Cunning. "I thought you trusted Connie implicitly."

Her expression threatened to rip out his heart. "So did I," she whispered. "I'm sorry."

"Me, too."

Despite traffic, they made the drive to Sacramento in just under three hours. She spent most of the drive dividing her time between Madam's cell phone and her sisters' until he finally confiscated them. To his intense satisfaction, she turned them over without a single objection. It was a gorgeous late spring day, bright and sunny, the roads reasonably clear of traffic. Blue and violet lupine and camas lilies covered the foothills, interspersed with spindles of lemon aster. Their destination took them off the beaten path, on to twisty roads that clung to the sides of rock-strewn cliffs, but offering breathtaking vistas of the mountains.

Luc touched the brakes as he rounded one of the hairpin turns and frowned. "How much farther, Téa?" he asked.

The sharpness in his tone had her head coming around. "What's wrong?"

He gave it to her straight. "The brakes are soft. I'm not sure how much longer they're going to hold. Look for a safe place we can turn off."

"This isn't a good section of road to have the brakes go out." Other than a thread of anxiety that underscored the comment, she remained impressively calm.

"No, it isn't."

He touched the brakes again, alarmed by the way the pedal depressed straight to the floor. They needed a pull-off and fast. Unfortunately, on Téa's side was sheer rock and on his side, an endless drop off the mountain. The car swept around the next bend and the speedometer inched ever higher. He pumped the brakes, hoping to rebuild enough pressure to stop the car. It didn't help, but he kept trying. And hoping.

"Hold on," he warned. "I'm going to use the engine to slow us."

Punching in the clutch, he downshifted. The car bucked, shimmied. He wrestled with the wheel, fighting to keep the car on the road. The back tires slid sideways and the engine screamed in protest. Another sharp curve loomed ahead and he took it wide, dragging the car through the gravel along the shoulder, hoping the extra friction would slow the car.

"I'm going to downshift again."

"I'm okay. Do it."

Her soothing voice acted like a balm. It eased his concerns about her and allowed him to give his full focus to the task at hand. He downshifted once again, wincing at the sound of gears clashing and grinding. If he stripped them, they'd really be in trouble. The road flattened out briefly and he used the opportunity to play with the emergency brake on the console between the two front seats. He pushed in the button on the end of the stick and eased it backward. The car slowed but fishtailed so badly he was forced to let go of the lever in order to control the car.

"I need your help," he said.

"Tell me what to do."

He waited until he successfully steered them around the next bend. "I need you to push in the button on the emergency brake handle and pull it backward until you feel resistance.

It'll engage the rear brakes. But if you yank too hard, I'll lose control. So do it gently."

Early afternoon daylight flickered through the trees, dancing across the grim determination that lined her face. She reached for the brake handle, the slight tremor of her hand giving away her agitation. She played with the brake, first too gently, then too much pressure, before finding that sweet spot between the two. They rounded another curve, taking it far too fast.

The next instant he saw it. A straight stretch of road lined with heavy brush on Téa's side. There were trees, as well, but they were a solid twenty feet off the road. He wouldn't get a better opportunity than this.

"I'm going to crash the car into the brush. Cover your face."

She limited herself to a single word. "Damn."

Skidding onto the gravel-covered shoulder, he dragged the passenger side of the car against the thick brush. Téa instinctively flinched away. Branches slashed against the metal, tearing at it, clawing at the vehicle. The car slowed and he arced more fully into the bushes. The wheel jerked from his hand and the car spun in a sharp 180, flinging itself into the embrace of the roadside shrubs before careening into a ditch and plowing sideways against a towering fir.

The scream of metal was followed by simultaneous explosions. The first, the ringing impact of tree against car, followed instantaneously by the bang of the airbags inflating. Fine powder filled the air causing his eyes and nose to sting. The coating from the airbags, no doubt. Or maybe the sting came from the impact of the bags, themselves. It all happened too fast for him to be certain. He remembered the sensation from his last car wreck, though, and shied from the memory. Silence hung in the air, broken by the wheeze of the engine and the whirr of one of the tires that continued to spin.

"Téa?" Luc cut the engine. The car was tilted, driver side down and her weight sagged against him. "Are you hurt?"

To his relief she shifted. "I . . . I'm okay. I think. Dizzy."

"Did you hit your head?"

"I don't know." She felt for it. "Small bump on the side."

"The back windows blew out. Are you cut? Can you tell?"

Her sigh sounded amazingly normal. "To be honest, I can't see a damn thing. My eyes are watering from all this dust."

"Hang on." He shoved the deflated airbags out of the way until he uncovered Téa. "Hello, gorgeous."

She managed a smile. "That bad?"

"That good."

He eased a wealth of curls away from her face. He'd never seen a more beautiful sight. Unable to help himself, he leaned in and kissed her. Inhaled her. Allowed himself a full minute to lose himself in celebration that they'd survived such a close call. She wound her arms around his neck and kissed him back with gratifying enthusiasm. Finally, he pulled away and cupped her face, his fingers skating gingerly over her face and into her hair. He found the bump she'd indicated, saw her wince and skimmed past it as he checked the rest of her.

"If we manage to get out of this with only a small bump and a batch of scrapes and bruises, we can consider it a miracle."

"No, the miracle is that you were behind that wheel instead of me," she replied. "If I'd been on my own—" She broke off with a shudder.

Luc's eyes narrowed and he filed the comment away for future consideration. "Any chance you can open your door? Mine's wrapped around the tree."

"I'll try." She squirmed around, wedging her shapely backside against him while she fumbled with the door. "It's too heavy. I can't lift it."

"Okay. How about you dig out one of your cell phones so we can call for help?"

"I'm not sure where my purse ended up."

He shifted, fighting back a curse when his knee issued a sharp complaint. Great. Just what he needed. He poked around the floor of the car until he found her bag and passed it over.

"Everything's jumbled," she murmured. "Okay, here's one. Oh. It's our phone."

For some reason the comment gave him a warm, possessive feeling. "Perfect."

She placed the call and within twenty minutes the car swarmed with emergency personnel who extracted them in no time. While the EMTs examined Téa, Luc had a private conversation with one of the county deputies, whose nametag read Sandford. Together they walked the path the car had taken and the deputy shook his head in disbelief.

"That's one hell of a piece of driving. I think you picked the only stretch on this road where you could have gotten away with ditching the car the way you did." Sandford gestured farther down the road. "If you'd kept going you'd have ended up driving right off the mountainside.

Sorry to say, I've seen the results of that once before. Just as soon never see it again."

"Not much choice but to ditch. The brakes went out on me."

"Bad place to have that happen."

It would have been just as bad if they'd taken the coast road Conway had requested, Luc realized. Long sections were a steep drop into the Pacific on one side and a wall of rock on the other. "I want the car checked from top to bottom." Luc spared a glance over his shoulder and grimaced. "At least, what's left of it."

Sandford's eyebrows shot upward. "You think someone messed with the brakes?"

"Let's just say I want to cover all the bases."

"I'll have it impounded, Mr. Dante."

"And the less said to Ms. de Luca, the better."

Sandford shrugged. "Nothing to tell her. Yet." He jerked his head in the direction of the ambulance. "I suggest you get that leg checked out. We're not big enough to warrant an actual hospital, but we have a decent medical center down the road a piece. They're going to want to transport you there to get checked out and I advise you let them."

Luc didn't have the energy to argue, though the next few hours weren't the most pleasant he'd ever experienced. After a battery of tests, they were finally released. They discovered Sandford had rescued their belongings from the mangled remains of the car and dropped them off at the medical center. Téa took the time to send text messages to her sisters letting them know she'd arrived safely—"safely" being a relative term. She was careful not to mention the accident. On their way out the door, one of the nurses recommended they spend the night at a nearby bed-and-breakfast rather than the local mom-and-pop motel while they arranged for transportation home.

The proprietress welcomed them with open arms and tutted over their accident. Then she insisted on giving them her best accommodations, a honeymoon cabin tucked under a stand of pines and overlooking a small, private lake.

"Nothing better to ease your aches and pains than a view from the back deck. And if that's not enough, there's a hot tub out there that will do the trick. Just had it put in. You two will be the first to give it a whirl."

"Sounds like heaven," Téa admitted with a weary smile.

The two of them limped down the path toward the lake. Luc unlocked the door and shoved himself and their bags over the threshold. Téa made a beeline toward the bedroom, and of more interest, the king-size bed. Kicking off her shoes, she dropped face-first onto the mattress.

"Come on," she mumbled around the feather pillow. "There's enough room here for a small army."

He didn't need a second invitation. He invaded the bed, an army of one, scooped Téa into his arms and was asleep before she'd finished spooning that glorious backside up against his thighs.

Chapter Seven

Téa surfaced slowly, aware of a delicious warmth surrounding her and an intense feeling of peace and security, both of which made her reluctant to open her eyes in case it caused the sensation to vanish. She might have drifted back to sleep if Luc hadn't stirred.

"Damn knee," he muttered.

Instantly she sat up and twisted to face him. "What can I do?"

He massaged the joint. "Just need to take an anti-inflammatory."

"Would soaking in the hot tub help?"

Early evening sunshine slipped through the shaded window and highlighted the grin creasing his face. He regarded her speculatively, the color of his eyes a sleep-laden tawny gold, filled with the sort of hunger that caused her heart rate to kick up a tad.

"It would help, but only if you join me."

Her concern eased and an answering smile flirted with her mouth. "How would my being there help your knee?"

"It would take my mind off the pain," he offered hopefully.

"No doubt." She escaped the bed and winced. Bruises she hadn't known she possessed made themselves known. "Maybe it'll take both of our minds off the pain."

His amusement vanished. "Where do you hurt? Do we need to go back to the medical center?"

"No, no," she reassured. "A few scrapes and bruises. They warned me it would get worse before it got better. I think a soak in a hot tub is just what the doctor ordered."

"First food. We skipped lunch, if you recall."

"Sounds good. But no alcohol for twenty-four hours."

"Spoilsport." He yawned. "I wonder if there's anywhere around here that delivers."

"I'll call the front desk and ask."

There was a nearby pizza place and, after calling in an order, Téa closeted herself in the bathroom for a quick shower. She wasn't surprised when Luc joined her. He wrapped his arms around her and drew her against his chest.

She tilted her head back and relaxed against him.

"You shouldn't be here."

Somehow he'd found the soap and traced her curves with slick, sudsy hands. "Or doing this?"

She moaned. "Probably not. The pizza is due to arrive any minute."

He nuzzled the sensitive skin in the curve of her neck. "Do you want to eat it in the hot tub?"

She sank against him in clear surrender. "Probably be better than eating it in the shower."

They never made it to the hot tub. The minute Luc paid off the delivery boy, they carried the pizza to the bedroom. Téa climbed into his lap and fed him a slice while helping herself to one, as well. Somehow the box ended up on the floor, along with the terry cloth robes they'd found hanging on the back of the bathroom door.

She feathered a string of kisses from shoulder to mouth. "We weren't supposed to do this again, not while we were working together," she reminded him.

He settled her more firmly on his lap. "I won't tell, if you don't."

"Works for me."

He rolled her under him and gave her his close and undivided attention. She was soft and sweet from her shower, though the bruises she'd sustained from the car crash were already purpling her ivory skin. He kissed each and every one, wishing he could kiss away the hurt as easily. It horrified him, how close they'd come.

"If you hadn't been there . . ." Her words echoed his thoughts.

"But I was."

"Have I thanked you, yet, for saving my life?"

"That's not nec—"

He never finished his sentence. She inhaled the last word, drinking him in, and he sank into the mattress with her. Sank into her mouth, over her body, and into the warmth and passion she so openly offered. The Inferno hummed between them, a livewire quietly pulsating no matter how far apart they were. But here, in her arms, in this bed together, it crackled with a deep and abiding need that drove him to possess the woman he considered his and his alone.

It was temporary, he reminded himself. He wasn't made for love or marriage or commitment. The accident five years ago had brought that fact home. But somehow, in this moment out of time, it seemed less imperative.

He sculpted her shape with his hands, lingering over the sleek, toned curves. "So perfect," he murmured.

"Funny. I was going to say the same about you."

She pushed at his shoulders and obliging, he rolled onto his back. She drifted over him. Delicately. Tenderly. Massaged the tension from his arms and shoulders, then ran her fingertips across his chest. Just the lightest of touches. Sheer torture. He reached for her, but she pushed him away.

"No. Not yet. I'm not through," she protested.

"I am." Heaven help him. "Or I will be if you don't stop."

"And here I thought you were such a tough guy," she teased.

"Hell," he muttered. "So did I."

Her laugh whispered in the gathering dark. "Then, control yourself, tough guy."

She continued along her path of destruction, wreaking havoc with each new caress. He sucked in air, his hands fisting in the sheets so they wouldn't fist in her hair and yank her back into his arms. And still she continued, drifting ever lower until she found the rigid length of him.

There she paused. There she lingered. There she took him, as he'd once taken her. It was beyond intimate. Beyond glorious. Beyond thought and description. He'd never fully surrendered to a woman before, never lost control of what happened in bed. Never felt safe enough to let go of that final shred of containment. But something about Téa . . .

Something about this woman loosened all he'd kept wrapped up tight. Something about her slipped beneath his guard and allowed her to breach every last one of his defenses. He could feel her within him. He drew her in with every breath. Felt her sweep through his veins with every beat of his heart. Felt her feminine strength and power to the very marrow of his bones. Held her in a soul-deep grip that he'd never willingly let go.

He called to her, his voice hoarse and desperate. And she answered him, giving of herself in the most generous way possible. He didn't hold back. Couldn't. Afterward, they curled together, locked tight within each other's embrace.

He regained consciousness hours later while dark lay full around them. He eased into her, waking her in the sweetest way possible. She sighed in pleasure, wrapping him up as he gave all he had to her. Driving the storm that swirled within them before riding with her on the wild wind that swept them away.

Then once again they slept, two parts made whole.

"No!"

Téa jerked upright at the visceral shout, her heart pounding. "Luc?"

Beside her, he twisted in the bedcovers, clearly in the throes of a nightmare. "I won't do it!"

She caught her bottom lip between her teeth, not quite certain whether or not she should touch him, in case he hit out in panic. She'd read somewhere of that possibility. Instead she scooted to the far side of the bed and called to him. "Luc. Wake up. You're dreaming."

"Got to stop the bleeding."

She flinched. "Luc." This time she raised her voice, speaking firmly. "Wake up. Now."

To her relief, he came to. Unlike her, he didn't jump up, but froze, swiftly assessing the situation before his tension slackened. He scrubbed a hand across his face. "Aw, hell."

"Bad dream?" she asked in as neutral a voice as possible.

"Yeah." He levered up on one elbow, squinting at the bedside table. "Can you see what time is it?"

"A little before eight." She hesitated. "Do you want to talk about it?"

He spared her a brief glance. "Do you suppose that hot tub is still up and running?"

He hadn't answered her question. Then again, maybe he had. "Should be."

He caught her hand in his and tugged. "Can't hurt to find out."

They snatched up their bathrobes on the way to the back porch where the sun peeked over the mountaintops and skipped across the stillness of the lake. In the distance, a loon gave a startled cry, the eerie sound echoing over the water. Other than the birds and deer, the place was deserted, protected from curious eyes by a tall privacy fence. They removed the cover from the hot tub and draped their robes across a nearby bench. Shivering from the morning mountain chill, they climbed into the gently steaming water.

To Téa's amusement they both sighed in unison as they sank into the warmth. Luc pushed a button on the inset panel next to him and the water gently churned around them. Satisfied, he scooped her close, settling her in the vee of his legs. She relaxed against his chest.

It was as though she'd been gifted with a taste of heaven and she savored the unexpected moment. They sat for a while in peaceful silence, simply enjoying the view and each other.

Then Téa gathered up her courage and said, "I have nightmares, too." She waited a second before continuing. "Not . . . not just bad dreams. But waking-up-screaming, in-a-total-sweat type night terrors."

"Sounds familiar. Your parents?" It didn't surprise her that he was so quick to pinpoint the cause.

"Yes." The word was barely audible over the sound of the jets. "It was my fault, you know."

"What happened?" For some reason, the simple question sliced neatly through the scars, straight down to the source of the infection.

"I went to a party I'd been forbidden to attend. They found out and tracked me down. They were on the sidewalk outside, approaching the house when one of the girls started screaming that we were about to get busted. The boy I was with jumped in his car. He was drunk, of course." She shrugged. "It was over in an instant. He didn't see them, they couldn't get out of the way in time."

"I'm sorry."

"Aren't you going to tell me it wasn't my fault?"

"You already know that," he startled her by saying. "But I understand now why you've taken on the role of mother to your stepsisters. Why you feel obligated to put your family ahead of your own needs and wants. I can't see you doing anything else. Not until you're ready to forgive yourself."

Tears flooded her eyes and she blinked hard to hold them at bay. "What about you? What are you blaming yourself for?"

Luc sighed. "Takes one to know one?"

"Something like that." She made an educated guess. "I gather this is in some way related to your injured knee?"

"Yeah. Same incident."

She turned, curled into him, rested her cheek against his chest while the water frothed around them. It felt right to be with him, held like this. "Must have been bad if you still have nightmares about it."

He held on to her as though she anchored him against the pull and drag of a turbulent sea. "Five years bad."

She winced. "If you'd rather not—"

"You did. Seems only fair that I should, too." He took another minute to gather himself. "I owned my own security firm after I left the military. We specialized in personal protection."

"Dangerous."

"Boring," he corrected, "with the occasional splash of terrifying."

"Got it. This must have been one of the terrifying episodes."

"This was the terrifying episode."

"What went wrong?" Because, clearly, something had.

"There was a married couple. Sonya and Kurt Jorgen." She felt him swallow. "They had a young child, maybe five. Kurt asked me to help them disappear for a while. I knew something wasn't quite right. Hell, my internal alarm system went haywire even during that first meeting. I questioned him, but he kept insisting they wanted to reconsider the direction they were taking in life and just needed to get away from it all for a while."

She had to agree with Luc. Something didn't add up. "How did Kurt explain the need for a bodyguard?"

"He claimed to have a lot of money. That taking off would leave him vulnerable. He just wanted some protection until they settled in somewhere. Mainly, he wanted me to show him how to get lost for a couple months."

"But that wasn't the real problem." She didn't phrase it as a question.

"Hell, no. It turns out the husband witnessed an incident at work he shouldn't have, but neglected to mention that detail when he hired me. On the way to disappearing, goons of Kurt's employer caught up with us and ran us off the road. I failed to do then what I succeeded in doing yesterday."

"A controlled crash," she murmured numbly.

"A controlled crash. The husband was killed instantly." She felt the harsh swallow again. Heard the choke in the rumble of words. "The kid, too. Sonya was badly hurt. The goons managed to take themselves out at the same time they took us out. Since they weren't a problem, I worked on saving Sonya."

"She died, too?"

"No. I saved her." He waited a beat before dropping the other shoe. "Unfortunately, she didn't want to be saved. She begged me to let her die so she could be with her husband and son."

Téa tightened her grip, wrapped him up in as much warmth as she could muster, hanging on tight. "Oh, Luc."

He relaxed into her embrace, though she could feel the emotional walls he erected pushing at her, trying to hold her at a distance. "When I visited the wife in the hospital, she became so hysterical they had to sedate her. She just kept screaming at me that she hated me. That I should have let her die."

"I'm so sorry. She was out of her mind with grief." Téa tilted her head back to look up at him. "You must realize that?"

"Of course I realize it. Just as I realize it wasn't my fault when she attempted to take her own life three months later." His voice grew even more grim, if that were possible. "Didn't succeed."

"What ultimately happened to her?"

"I have no idea." He closed his eyes and shook his head. "I'm afraid to find out."

"You think she's gone, don't you?"

He shrugged. When he opened his eyes again, they were the darkest she'd ever seen. Hard. Remote. Dispassionate. "If you're that determined to die, chances are excellent you'll eventually succeed."

"You did the right thing. You do understand that, don't you?" she asked urgently. "It wasn't your fault."

He didn't bother to point out the irony of her statement. "Trust me, I've looked at this from every possible direction. If the husband had warned me when he first hired me. If I'd hit the brakes sooner. Later. Turned left instead of right." He shrugged dismissively. "The bottom line is, I took the job. People died. End of story. Afterward, I dissolved the business and went to work for Dantes Courier Service."

But it wasn't. She could see it wasn't. The incident had struck hard and deep, and left wounds that still hadn't healed, just as hers hadn't. "What aren't you telling me?"

He looked at her with tarnished eyes, the expression so distant. So emotionless. "I don't know what you're talking about."

She shivered despite the warmth of the water. "Yes, you do." She'd never been more certain of anything in her life. "Something else happened that day. What was it?"

He hesitated, then offered a cool smile. "Okay, fair enough. It wasn't part of the accident, merely a decision I made as a result of it. Just like you made the decision to fill in for your parents."

Every feminine instinct she possessed warned her to let it go. To change the direction of the conversation. To offer some lighthearted quip that would cut through the thickening tension. But she couldn't. Wouldn't. Not while that look of pain and grief darkened Luc's eyes. Not while the poison still swept through his veins, infecting every aspect of his life. Not while her palm itched and throbbed, warning that whatever existed between them would always be tainted by the hideous events of that day.

"Go on," she whispered. "Tell me what you decided."

"I decided that I'd never marry."

With that, he shifted her to one side and erupted from the hot tub. He padded across the deck like some great, sleek jungle cat to where they'd discarded their robes. He shrugged into his and held the other out to her.

"I gather we're done soaking?" she asked in a neutral voice.

"Since this is a bed-and-breakfast, I thought we'd go and find the breakfast portion of our stay. According to my stomach, that pizza is a fond but distant memory."

Téa didn't bother arguing. One look at Luc's face convinced her of that. She switched off the jets and hurried from the steaming warmth of the tub into the protective covering of her robe, doing her best to limit her exposure to the crisp mountain air. Luc opened the French doors that led into the living area of the cabin and picked up the phone. Téa waited while he spoke to the owner.

"It would seem that one of the benefits of the honeymoon cabin is private dining," he explained once he'd hung up. "They'll bring breakfast to us."

"I guess we should dress."

"Then I need to arrange for a rental car. We should also decide if we're staying another night or returning to the city."

He spoke calmly, as though his earlier announcement was of little concern. Maybe it wasn't to him. But she'd always been hampered by a logical nature and she didn't understand the connection between the two incidents. Deciding to bide her time, she returned to the bedroom to dress. Luc was on the phone arranging for a car to be brought in from Lake Tahoe when a staff member arrived with a loaded tray.

"There's a coffee machine in the kitchenette," he informed Téa. "I'll start a fresh pot for you. Or would you prefer tea?"

"Coffee is fine," Téa confirmed.

As soon as the coffee finished brewing, she and Luc took their breakfast onto the deck. The temperature had crept upward, warmed by the sunshine splashing down from a cloudless sky. They fell on their meal as though they hadn't eaten in a week, polishing off every bite before relaxing in their chairs to enjoy a steaming cup of coffee.

"Go on," Luc surprised her by saying. "Ask."

She didn't bother pretending. There wasn't any point. Plus, she suffered from the small matter of being, quote, the world's worst liar, end quote. "Fine. I'll ask." She tried for an indifferent attitude, as though she couldn't care less. She suspected she failed miserably at the attempt. "What has the accident got to do with your decision to never marry?"

He hesitated. "You have to understand my world. The Dante world," he offered on a roundabout way. "Primo and Nonna. My parents. My uncle and his disaster of a marriage."

Téa lifted a shoulder. "I'm sorry. I'm not following." Her brows drew together. "Wait. Is this about The Inferno?"

"Yes." He refilled his coffee cup and topped off hers. "All my life I've heard about The Inferno. Lived with The Inferno. Had it stuffed down my throat."

Téa attempted a light laugh. "Luc, it's just a story. A charming family legend."

He shook his head. "It's more than legend for the Dantes. You've seen my grandparents. They'll turn eighty soon and they still can't keep their hands off each other. My parents aren't any better. Nor are my cousins. And every last one of them claims it's because of this damn Inferno."

"What about your uncle?" Téa strove for normalcy. "You said his marriage was a disaster. Doesn't that prove The Inferno doesn't always work?"

He laughed without humor. "Uncle Dominic proves just the opposite. You see, he didn't marry for love, even though he was madly in love with one of his jewelry designers and had a torrid affair with her. Instead he married Aunt Laura for her money. Primo warned it would end in disaster. And it did. Uncle Dom and my aunt were killed years ago in a boating accident while in the throes of a divorce discussion. I gather he'd decided to marry this jewelry designer, after all. When my aunt and uncle died, my grandparents took in Sev and my cousins and raised them."

So much tragedy! "Oh, Luc. I'm so sorry."

"Of course, that only solidified the legend in everyone's eyes. Turned your charming fairy tale into truth."

"But it's not," she insisted.

He reached across the table and took her hand in his, intertwined their fingers so their palms met and mated. "Isn't it?"

She shuddered. "I—" She snatched an uneven breath. "What we're experiencing is just a bad case of physical attraction. Anything else would be illogical."

"I'm glad to hear you say that. Because that's what it's going to stay," he warned, even as a spark of desire caught hold and roared to life. "I won't be forced into a marriage I don't want because of a make-believe fairy tale."

"No one is forcing you to do anything," she protested.

"Aren't they?" He released her and sat back. A hint of cynicism played about his mouth and burnished his eyes. "Maybe it would have occurred to me sooner if I hadn't been so distracted. But there's a lot that doesn't add up. For instance, why have I been hired as your bodyguard?"

She offered a self-deprecating smile. "Apparently because I can't put one foot in front of the other without tripping over it."

"Funny." He cocked his head to one side. "In the couple of weeks we've spent together, I haven't noticed that about you."

"The first time we met—" she began.

"Had me worried," he agreed with a nod. "But how many incidents have there been since?"

"Well, none," she admitted. "But I assumed that was because you were there." She broke off with a frown. "Now that I say it out loud it doesn't make the least bit of sense, does it?"

"No, it doesn't. I've just recently concluded there's only one reason we were brought together."

She gave a disbelieving laugh. "You can't think it's because of The Inferno. How could anyone possibly know we'd be a match?"

Luc lifted his cup and stared at her over the rim, his gaze enigmatic through the steam. "That stopped me, too, until it occurred we met once before, remember?"

"Ages ago," she said with a dismissive wave of her hand. "We were children."

"Really? Lazz and Ariana first met as children. Primo claims Uncle Dominic saw early signs of The Inferno even then. As a result, he and Ariana's father contracted a marriage between them right then and there."

Téa's mouth opened, then shut again, before she managed to say, "You must be joking."

"Not even a little."

"And you suspect your parents or grandparents caught something similar between us? How is that possible?" she scoffed. "We hardly said two words to each other. We despised each other at first sight."

"Don't you remember why?"

"I . . ." She thought back, struggled to recall that miserable, uncomfortable summer. "You kept pestering me. Teasing me."

"Zapping you," he said softly.

"That's right. I remember now. It was like you were filled with static electricity. And you loved jumping out at me when I least expected it to give me a shock." Her eyes narrowed. "Brat."

"Think about it," he urged. "Wouldn't that be a gentler, more childish version of what we experienced when we first touched as adults?"

She drew back in her chair, closing in on herself. "I thought you didn't believe in The Inferno," she accused. "I don't."

"But my parents and grandparents, and I'm assuming Madam, believe implicitly."

Her eyes widened in outrage. "And because of that zapping . . ."

He nodded. "I'm now guessing they decided we were experiencing The Inferno. Primo made me stop and told me not to go near you for the rest of your visit. And when Primo lays down the law . . ." Luc lifted a shoulder. "So, the years passed. I'm willing to bet Nonna and Madam decided it was time to put us together again and see if anything happened between us. I'm also guessing they drummed up your distraction as the perfect excuse."

Téa returned her cup to the saucer with a sharp click. "Fine. Let's say for the sake of argument that the reason we're in our current predicament is because of what happened at the lake all those years ago. That certainly doesn't mean we have to act on it. And I still don't understand what The Inferno has to do with the car crash and your decision not to marry."

Darkness settled over him and she could tell he wasn't seeing her. She'd lost him to those long-ago events. "The Dantes believe once we're mated through The Inferno, it's a lifetime love affair. One man. One woman. One love."

"Isn't that the idea with all marriages, at least going in?" she asked gently.

He nodded. "That's how it was between the Jorgens. Even I could see that much, despite the limited amount of time we spent together. One second they were a loving family. The next she was alone. Her life ended when theirs did, but she still lived. Empty. Broken. And forced to remain that way for the rest of her life—a life she appeared determined to end."

Téa struggled to put the pieces he showed her into a logical whole. "And you're afraid that will happen to you?"

Luc focused on her. "Sonya gave every part of herself to Kurt and their son. When they were gone, she had nothing left. As far as she was concerned, without them her life ended. Someone just forgot to turn out the lights for her."

"Sonya isn't you," Téa argued.

"No, she isn't. Because I won't surrender that much of myself to another person. I watched Rafe do it with his wife, Leigh, and watched her gut him on her way out the door. I won't be another Sonya. I won't be Rafe after the death of his marriage." He turned his haunted gaze on her. "So, I won't marry."

Téa shook her head. "You're wrong, Luc. It's not that you won't marry. What you've decided is you won't love. Funny thing about love." She shoved her empty coffee cup aside. "You're assuming you have some control over it."

"I do."

"That's where you're wrong." She pushed back her chair and stood. "Unfortunately for you, love chooses. And it chooses whether you're willing or not."

With that Téa turned and forced herself to walk away from what she'd just discovered she wanted most in the world.

Chapter Eight

A couple hours later, the rental car was delivered and Luc signed the necessary papers to take possession. The owner of the bed-and-breakfast asked if they wanted the cabin for a second night and Luc glanced at Téa.

"It's your call," he said without expression.

Téa hesitated. "I don't know how long it'll take to locate the former manager of our plant and convince him to talk. Plus, Connie expects me to be gone at least two days, if not three. I'd rather he not find out I didn't go where he requested."

"There's weather moving in late this afternoon," the owner offered tentatively. "Don't want to be on these mountain roads when it hits. Should be clear again by tomorrow morning."

Téa gave a decisive nod. "We'll stay another night, if that's all right."

The owner beamed. "Our next reservation doesn't arrive until Friday. We'd be happy to have you until then."

Téa shook her head apologetically. "One more night should do it." She spared Luc a wistful glance, one that clearly told of her preference to remain for the entire week. The look—one that said a single word from him would be enough to have her prolong their stay—would have slayed a weaker man. He forced himself to remain impassive beneath it. She sighed. "There's a lot of work sitting on my desk. Plus, I have to replace my car."

No doubt an added expense and distraction she didn't need right now. "I'll help."

"That's not necessary," she replied with cool politeness.

"It's the least I can do considering I'm the one who crashed it," he replied just as politely.

She let it go and turned to address the owner who'd been watching their byplay with an indulgent expression. "Could you give me directions to the town of Polk?"

Luc waited patiently while the two women inched their way over Téa's cell phone GPS. A short time later they were on the road again. He shot her a fleeting glance. She appeared a shade paler than usual, her slight dusting of freckles standing out more sharply than usual, and she had a grim set to her mouth. More telling, her hands were laced together in a death grip, her knuckles bleached white.

Day Leclaire

"You okay?" he asked after the first series of hairpin turns. He'd deliberately kept their speed a full five miles beneath the posted limit.

"I'll survive."

"I don't doubt it for a minute."

They arrived in Polk shortly before noon and Luc suggested they have lunch before tackling the manager. Téa settled on a local café with boxes of colorful flowers outside and a homey setup inside. The menu offered a surprising variety of options and their lunch choices were attractively plated when they arrived.

"What's this guy's name you plan to visit?" Luc asked while they ate.

"Krendal. Douglas Krendal."

"Does he know you're coming?"

She hesitated. "I thought I'd surprise him. I called to make certain he was in. Pretended I was a telemarketer." She winced and rubbed her ear. "Mr. Krendal doesn't mince words."

"You may find that helpful when you talk to him."

"That's what I'm hoping." She hesitated, playing with her fork and pushing her lunch around her plate. "Listen, I want to speak privately with him. I suspect he'll be more open if it's just the two of us."

Luc cocked an eyebrow. "In other words, the conversation is none of my business?"

"Okay, yes."

"No problem."

"Really?" she asked skeptically. "You're not going to argue the way you have about Connie?"

He shrugged. "The situation with your cousin is different. I don't trust the guy. So, I've made a point of sticking close whenever he starts yanking on the puppet strings."

She stiffened. "I gather I'm the puppet?"

"Time will tell." He gestured toward her plate. "You done?"

"Yes." She shoved her half-eaten lunch to one side. "Let's get this over with."

They found the Krendal place without too much trouble, the cottage perched on top of one of the endless hillsides surrounding the town of Polk. It was a small rambler on a large piece of property, tucked beneath a towering stand of pine trees. Luc pulled into the driveway and parked along one edge of the small circle of gravel on the side of the house. Téa exited the car and followed the cement walkway to the front door. He watched while she knocked and the door opened. Saw her introduce herself and Krendal's grim resistance. Caught the instant it began to fade beneath Téa's warmth. At long last, the door swung wide and she disappeared inside.

His cell phone vibrated about five minutes into the wait and he checked the caller ID. "Yeah, Juice," he said by way of greeting. "What did you find out about Billings?"

"The man or the business?"

"Okay, now you've got my attention." Luc frowned as he listened, his frown deepening with each new revelation. "Well, hell," he said when Juice completed his report.

"That was my reaction. What are you going to tell the de Luca woman?"

"Everything."

"She's not going to be happy."

"Furious would be my guess."

"Glad you're the one handing her the news and not me."

"Chicken."

"Cluck-cluck." And with that, the line went dead.

Twenty minutes later Téa emerged from the house. She shook hands with Krendal and returned to the car, her heels rapping out a hard, staccato beat on the walkway leading to the gravel driveway. She climbed into the car and slammed the door closed. "That *bastard!*"

Luc folded his arms along the top of the steering wheel and assessed the level of her anger. If he were to guess, he'd say steaming, bordering on, "thar she blows." "I hope that comment's aimed at Cousin Connie and not Mr. Krendal," he said.

"Oh, it's definitely aimed at Cousin Connie. Or maybe I should say Cousin Con Artist." She gave an imperious wave of her hand. "Let's go. I need to drive off some of this mad."

Little did she know. "Okay."

He headed back toward their rental cabin in silence, giving her the opportunity to stew. Maybe once she'd come to terms with the information Krendal had dumped on her, she'd be in a better position to deal with his news. In the distance, the first evidence of the storm they'd been warned about boiled up over the tops of the nearby mountains, the clouds filled with threat and turmoil. They were a perfect punctuation mark to Téa's mood. He checked his watch, judged the distance and decided they'd get to the cabin with time to spare.

By the time they parked in front of the cabin, the sky had turned nighttime dark. Luc hustled Téa inside and flicked on lights to dispel the gathering gloom. While he went in search of a flashlight or candles in case the storm knocked out the power, Téa checked her various cell phones and frowned. "What's wrong?"

"No signal. I hope Madam and the girls aren't worried." She brightened. "Maybe they haven't tried to call."

He set out a sleeve of candles he found in one of the drawers in the kitchenette, along with a box of matches. "What do you suppose the odds are of that happening?"

Her hopeful mood vanished. "Zero to less than zero." She released a sigh. "I need a drink."

He opened the door to the small refrigerator. "You're in luck. It would seem the honeymoon cabin also comes with a complimentary bottle of champagne. Are we cleared to drink, do you suppose?"

Téa checked her watch and nodded. "We're just past the twenty-four-hour time frame we were given by the doctor."

"Good enough."

Luc pulled out the bottle and removed the foil and wire, before cautiously uncorking it. Digging through the cupboards, he unearthed a pair of Lucite flutes and poured them each a glass. Téa took a tentative swallow and wrinkled her nose at the explosion of bubbles.

"Surprisingly good," she said with a hint of surprise. "Is it a California wine?"

"Yes. Carneros region."

"That explains it." She drank another couple sips, stalling. Then finally, said, "There's something I need to tell you."

"About Krendal?"

She waved that aside. "No. It's about the night we were at Primo's for Rafe's birthday party."

He wondered when they'd get back to that. "I gather you're about to tell me the real reason you were so upset when we left. Why you suddenly decided to put all your focus on work and protecting your family."

"Yes." She spared him a speculative glance. "Sev never said anything to you?"

"No." And Sev would pay for that small oversight. "What happened?"

"Your cousin warned me there was a quality issue with our product."

He took a moment to absorb that, to put it together with the information Juice had provided. "I gather that explains your confrontation on Monday with Conway." Luc sampled the champagne, also approved it and topped off their glasses. "I can't wait to hear his explanation."

"He claimed it was all a huge error and he'd look into it."

"And you bought that?"

She waved her glass at him. "Don't be ridiculous. Of course I didn't buy it. The man is as bad a liar as I am."

Luc choked on a laugh. "Must run in the genes."

"No doubt. Anyway, he insisted I stay out of it and even when I pointed out that I'd be right in the middle of the fiasco in five short weeks—about a month now—he told me that was fine. In five short weeks I could handle it. In the meantime, he was in charge and he'd get in touch with Sev. As if that wasn't enough, he forbid me from contacting your cousin under any circumstances."

"That's when you came storming out and buried your nose in the spreadsheets."

"There was something about them . . ." Her eyes glittered darkly in the deepening gloom. "Once I understood the underlying problem, I knew what to look for."

"Your cousin has been cutting corners."

She nodded. "And charging more for an inferior product. That's what I didn't catch in the accounting records. You see, the price we charge our customers has gone up, but when I looked more carefully, our manufacturing costs have actually dropped, despite the fact our overall profit remains the same."

Even without an accounting background, Luc could add together those three numbers to equal something was definitely fishy. "If your manufacturing costs have gone down, your cost to customers increased, the profit margin should have skyrocketed."

"You would think," she agreed. "And the bottom line would have skyrocketed if our profit hadn't vanished into the cost of purchasing new equipment. On paper it appears legit."

"Huh."

She tilted her head to one side. "You look like a puzzle piece just fell into place."

"It did. First tell me what Krendal said, and then I'll explain."

"Okay." She helped herself to more champagne. "Douglas Krendal was the production manager of our manufacturing plant. He claims Connie forced him out."

"Because Krendal caught on to what Billings was doing," Luc guessed.

"Yes. And he expressed his disapproval in no uncertain terms. He'd worked for my grandfather for years and was outraged Connie wanted to cut corners by producing an inferior product."

"So, Conway fired him."

"Retired him," she corrected with a shrug. "But, essentially, you're right. He got rid of Douglas at the earliest opportunity."

Luc hesitated, knowing the time had come to give her the rest of the bad news. He blew out a breath. "You're not going to like this next part."

She stilled, a look of intense vulnerability sweeping across her face. "Please tell me you're not a secret operative for my cousin."

The sheer unexpectedness of her comment provoked a laugh. "No, I'm not a spy," he said tenderly. To his relief, his reassurance restored her confidence. "But I did ask the Dantes' head of security to dig into your cousin's background." He grimaced. "It's not good, Téa."

She sank into a nearby chair. "Let me have it."

"Essentially, he's broke."

Her mouth dropped open. "How is that possible? I happen to know what he makes running Bling and it's a pretty penny."

"Right, except he doesn't receive a percentage of the profits from the company the way he would if he were the owner. He's on salary with modest bonuses approved by the board. And he's been funneling all available funds into this new start-up business he's about to launch." He allowed that to sink in before adding, "There's more."

"Of course there is," she murmured.

"I think I know what he's up to."

"Is he embezzling?"

"Not funds." He waited a beat. "Equipment."

"The purchases he made with the profits." She frowned. "I don't understand. What does he want with the equipment?"

"This is sheer conjecture, but I'm pretty sure I'm right. I think he's going to start up a competing business." Téa inhaled sharply. "The poor quality merchandise—"

"—gets your customers angry. Makes them easier to steal away from Bling." Luc downed the last of his champagne and set the glass aside. "Oh, he's going to turn the family business over to you. He's just going to make sure it's nothing more than a shell when he does it. Then, when you're on the verge of bankruptcy because you've lost all your customers to him—"

"—he comes sweeping in and offers to buy me out for pennies on the dollar," she finished his sentence for him. "Connie's new start-up company then takes over the Billings name and he has everything my grandfather didn't leave him. The business, the name, and all the money."

"That's what I suspect."

"And I suspect you're right." She closed her eyes and thought about it. "The question is, what can I do to stop him? He's had ages to set all this up. I still don't take over for another four and a half weeks. He must know I'm close to figuring it out. Which means he has a full month to bring his plans to fruition while I watch helpless from the sidelines."

"He doesn't know you're on to him, yet," Luc attempted to reassure. "There's still time to do something."

Téa shook her head. "Not while he controls Bling. If I could just take over now . . ." She froze. Slowly her gaze shifted to fix on Luc. He didn't care for the speculative gleam in her eyes. "There is a way I can do that."

"Well, okay." He snatched up his glass, annoyed to find it empty. "Then do it."

"I need your help to put my plan into action."

A plan. Action. He was all over that. "You know I'm willing to do whatever I can."

She smiled. "I was hoping you'd say that."

For some reason, her expression worried him. It had turned calculating, filled with the same drive and determination he'd noticed the night of Rafe's birthday party.

"I'm almost afraid to ask, but what do you want me to do?"

"It's quite simple, really. I want you to marry me."

Luc stared at Téa in disbelief. "Excuse me?"

To her credit, she was smart enough to show a trace of nervousness. "You heard me." She gulped champagne. "I want you to marry me. Temporarily, of course."

"Oh, of course."

She flinched at his sarcasm. "Luc—"

He cut her off without hesitation. "I believe we had this discussion already." Anger ripped through him, accompanied by the first rumbling of the storm. "What part of 'I'm never going to get married' didn't you understand? The 'never' part or the 'married'?"

"Let me explain." She approached, showing either an impressive amount of bravery or proving just how badly she'd misjudged his current mood. "There's a clause in the will that says that if I marry, I inherit Billings outright, so long as I'm over the age of twenty-one."

"Outstanding. I wish you every success in finding someone to marry you."

"I don't think you understand."

"I understand perfectly," he snapped. "You're the one who doesn't understand. The answer, Ms. de Luca, is not just no, but *hell* no."

"I'll try not to be offended by that." A matching anger flared to life in her eyes, while outside lightning flashed, causing the electricity to sputter. "Don't you see? It's the perfect solution for both of us, Luc."

He folded his arms across his chest. "Okay, this I have to hear. How is marrying you the perfect solution for me?"

"Your entire family believes we've been struck by The Inferno, right?"

"Unfortunately."

"So, we give them what they want." Thunder crashed overhead and she had to wait for it to die down before continuing. "We give them a wedding between Inferno soul mates. A couple months down the road, say six or seven, we inform everyone it didn't work out. We divorce."

"Dantes don't divorce."

"Rafe did," she retorted, stung.

"Technically, he's a widower."

That stopped her. "Oh. I didn't realize. I'm sorry."

"You don't need to apologize to me."

She waved that aside. "We're getting off track here."

"I understand where you're going with this, Téa. I recommend you let it go."

Luc turned his back on her and crossed to stare out into the stormy darkness. A bolt of lightning streaked overhead, the reflection forking across the surface of the lake, while thunder boomed, the echo from it bouncing off the surrounding mountains. He could see the logic of her suggestion, just as he could see all the dangerous pitfalls along the way.

Pitfalls like the itch of The Inferno that would only grow stronger and burrow deeper with each additional day in her company. Pitfalls like having her in his bed and discovering he couldn't bring himself to let her go. Pitfalls like pregnancy. Or love.

He could see her reflection mirrored in the glass of the French door, picked up on her tension from the set of her shoulders and the way she fiddled with her empty flute. Despite his anger, he still wanted her, could feel the unwelcome connection pulsating between them.

With a sigh, he turned to face her. "You think if we marry, wait a reasonable amount of time and then claim it didn't work out, my family will leave me alone. Stop forcing this nonsense about The Inferno down my throat. Is that your plan?"

She nodded eagerly. "Exactly. Since they believe I'm your Inferno bride, they won't keep nagging you about marrying again."

"No." He folded his arms across his chest. "They'll just keep nagging me about getting back together with you."

"Oh." She sighed. "I hadn't thought of that."

He smiled dryly at the bitter disappointment in her voice. "That's because you don't know my family."

She was quick to regroup. "Well, when I marry for real that will put an end to it, won't it? They'll leave both of us alone."

He stilled. "Marry for real?"

"It's possible." She lifted her chin. "More than possible. Because unlike you I'm not afraid of love. Seeing your family, seeing how happy the various couples are, it's made me think. Maybe once my family is safe and financially secure, I can fall in love and get married, too. Start a family like Kiley and Francesca."

For an endless moment he couldn't think straight. Couldn't breathe. Images filled his head of Téa, heavy with a baby. His baby. And then the image shifted. Twisted. And suddenly it wasn't his baby any longer, but another man's.

Her husband's. A man who had the right to put his hands on her. To take her to his bed. To share every intimacy with her.

To give her a baby.

He heard a low snarl fill the room, barely aware it had been ripped from his throat. One minute he stood silhouetted by the pounding storm and the next he was across the room. He reached for her, swept her into his arms.

"Luc," she gasped. "What are you doing."

"You're the one with all the answers. You figure it out."

Luc reached the bed in fewer than a dozen limping steps and dropped Téa to the mattress. He followed her down, his mouth closing over the questions trembling on her lips. He had no memory of stripping off her clothes, of stripping away his own. Thunder crashed around them while lightning bleached the ebony from the night. He had a quick flash of Téa, a stunning palate of ivory splayed across a canvas of black. Only her hair and eyes offered any color, a spill of vibrant, fiery red, and a blue-green as deep and mysterious as the ocean.

The elements tore across the night, setting flame to the explosive passions trapped within the room. They came together, a clash of masculine and feminine that somehow found a melding point, a place where they joined with undeniable perfection and became one. Their bodies mated, moving to the rhythm of the storm, echoing its power and ferocity, giving no quarter and expecting none. They followed each other into the very heart of the tempest, riding it, driven by it to an exquisite climax.

Luc felt Téa peak, heard her cry of pleasure. That was all it took. He followed her up and over. He heard his name on her lips. Answered the cry with one of his own, with her name, the sound of it a stamp of possession. It grounded him as nothing else could have. Slowly the tumult calmed. And when it finished, he gathered her close. Gently. Tenderly. Safe within the harbor of his arms.

She pressed close, twining herself around him until he couldn't tell where she began and he ended. He simply held her, felt the steady beat of her heart filling his palm.

And he slept.

Téa woke the next morning feeling better than she had in her entire life. She had no idea what had gotten into Luc. He hadn't given her much opportunity to ask. But she could only hope it happened again. And soon. She stretched, feeling the pull of well-worked muscles, along with the twinge of lingering bruises.

Luc stirred and groaned. "Is the hot tub still out there?"

She snuggled, finding his warmth, pleased when he dropped a powerful arm over her and tucked her in close. "It's there unless it washed away in the storm."

"Is it still raining?"

"I don't hear anything. And I think that yellow stuff coming in through the drapes is sunshine."

"Okay. Just this once I'll let you carry me out to the hot tub. But only this once."

"I'll get right on that." She paused. "Are we there, yet?"

He pulled back slightly and frowned down at her. "You're not very good at this. Considering the number of times I've hauled you around, the least you could do is return the favor."

"Very inconsiderate of me," she said apologetically.

"I'll say." He escaped the bed and dragged her out, protesting all the way. "Come on. Let's go soak before we pack up."

"What about our robes?"

"Let them find their own hot tub."

Moving quickly, they stripped off the cover and climbed into the tub, allowing the heat and swirling jets of water to ease sore muscles. Téa stirred, picking up on an odd noise coming from the interior of the cabin. "I think I hear something." She sat up and craned her neck, thought better of it and ducked lower in the water. "What if it's one of the staff members with our breakfast?" she whispered frantically.

Luc grinned. "Then someone's going to be really embarrassed. And I'm willing to bet it won't be me."

She heard it then. Heard the voices coming closer. Voices that shouldn't be here. She had a whole two seconds to stare wild-eyed at Luc before Madam stepped onto the deck, followed closely by Téa's three stepsisters. Her grandmother's distinctive voice cut across the peaceful serenity of the morning. *"Madre del Dio!* Girls, don't look!"

But of course, they did.

Chapter Nine

Luc opened the door of the rental car and waited until Téa slid in before closing it. Then he limped around to the driver's side and climbed behind the wheel. He didn't start the engine.

"How did Madam find us?" he asked abruptly.

Téa answered readily enough. "Apparently the claims adjuster at my insurance agency called the house with a few more questions about the wrecked car. Madam took the call and then tried to get hold of me. When she couldn't—remember the service went out?—she assumed the worst. That we'd been injured in the accident." She rolled her eyes. "Though how I was well enough to call the insurance company but too badly injured to speak to her, I have no idea. Madam's not always the most logical person in the world." She paused. Flinched. "Oh, dear. I'll bet she was remembering the night my parents died."

"That still doesn't explain how she found us."

Téa shrugged, preoccupied with settling her shoulder bag and fastening her seatbelt. "I guess from the insurance company. If you recall I had to provide the claims adjuster with the location of the car. He must have passed that information on to Madam. She probably called the nearest medical facility. I know I would have. From there it would be a short hop to this place." She paused, studying him with a growing frown. "What's with the third degree?"

"Let's just say that her showing up and catching us naked in a hot tub is a bit too convenient for my taste," he said in a detached voice.

"Convenient? *Convenient!*" Téa leaned in, enunciating carefully. "For your information, Luciano Dante, there was absolutely nothing convenient about what just went down in that cabin this morning."

Time would tell. "How bad was it?" he asked.

She sat back, but he could see she continued to simmer. "I'm guessing about as bad as your conversation with Primo."

"Damn."

"Oh, yeah." She released a long sigh. "What did your grandfather have to say?"

He watched her closely, interested in her reaction. "He said we're now officially engaged."

Téa's eyes widened in shock. "Tell me you're joking."

"I'd love to. Unfortunately, I'm not. I'm open to any suggestions you might have for getting us out of this mess."

"Okay, here's one. Tell your grandfather no."

"That'll work." He turned the key in the ignition and the engine started with an extra roar, echoing his own irritation. "Not."

"So, that's it?" she asked. "Now we just get married?"

"Isn't that what you wanted?"

"Well, yes, but not like this." She folded her arms across her chest. "Be reasonable, Luc. It's not like anyone can force you to marry me."

"Oh, really? And what did Madam have to say after catching us naked in a hot tub after a night of raw passion?" He cupped a hand to his ear. "What's that? I can't hear you."

"I said . . ." Téa cleared her throat. "She's disappointed."

"Me, too. I had plans for that hot tub."

"She also said it was so unlike me. Selfish. Impulsive. And worst of all, I was setting a bad example for the girls."

"I'd have said it was exactly like you. Generous. Inventive. And those three witches you call sisters don't need any help riding their broomsticks to Badville. I'd say they invented the place. Especially Goth Girl."

"That's Katrina. It's just a phase."

"Scary."

"She's not scary. She's wonderful. All my sisters are wonderful."

"Particularly the one who would have stuck her tongue down my throat if you'd left us alone for a minute longer than you did." He shot Téa a quelling look when she opened her mouth to argue. "Don't tell me. I shouldn't take it personally. She's like that with all the men."

"Davida's naturally exuberant," she retorted, stung.

"Exuberant. That's a catchy name for it. Well, Vida's exuberance came across loud and clear."

Téa closed her mouth again and released a long, tired sigh. Luc winced. He felt like the worst kind of bully. It wasn't her fault that her stepsisters were hellions. Or that they hadn't received the right sort of discipline, though Téa had chosen to shoulder the blame for that, as well as the death of her parents.

"You know, there's an easy way out of this mess," he suggested.

"Which is?"

"We drop your sisters off at Primo and Nonna's. My grandparents will have them straightened out within a week. Then we gag and tie Cousin Connie and hide him in a dusty closet somewhere so you can start running Bling the minute we return."

She offered a reluctant smile. "And what about our impending nuptials? How do you propose we handle that small detail?"

"Huh." He frowned. "Okay, you got me there. I don't have a clue how to handle it."

"I do."

"Great. Why didn't you say so."

"I'll speak to Primo when we get back to San Francisco. Explain how everyone leapt to the wrong conclusions."

"Wrong conclusion," he repeated. "Naked plus hot tub equals not much of a leap."

Téa grimaced. "It also didn't help that the owner told Madam we were in the honeymoon cottage. At first, she assumed we'd eloped. When she found out we hadn't . . ."

"I gather the conversation went downhill from there."

"Oh, yeah."

Luc's cell phone rang and he dug it out of his pocket and tossed it to Téa. "See who that is, will you?"

She flipped open the phone and checked the caller ID. "It's Primo."

"Perfect. Go ahead and answer it. You can explain to him why we're not getting married."

"Okay," she agreed, though she didn't sound quite as sure of herself as she had earlier. "Hi, Primo, it's Téa. Yes, Luc is still with me. But he's driving, so—" She listened at length, tossing in several, uh-huhs and oh, dears.

"Tell him!" Luc encouraged.

She waved him silent. "Uh-huh. Oh, dear." She cleared her throat. "The thing is, Primo, Luc and I . . . Well, we don't want to get married. Right. I understand. Okay. No, you're right. Lake Tahoe isn't all that far."

"What the hell are you saying?" Luc bit out. "Just tell him no and hang up!"

"Excuse me a moment, Primo." She covered up the phone. "Would you please try not to wreck another car? If you can't drive straight, pull over. You're making me very nervous."

"I'm making you nervous? Give me that phone!"

"He doesn't want to talk to you. He wants to talk to me. Yes, Primo, I'm still here." Her eyes widened and she inhaled sharply. "Um. You're sure they're planning to print that? You do understand we don't want to get married, right? I made that clear? No, no. That's fine. I guess we'll see you tomorrow. Yes, I'll be sure to tell Luc. Bye."

Jamming on the brakes, Luc swung onto a pull-off on the side of the road and cut the engine. "So?" he demanded. "Did you tell him?"

Téa's head bobbed up and down. "Oh, I told him. Didn't you hear me tell him? I told him flat-out that we didn't want to get married."

"And he accepted that?"

She squirmed. "Sort of."

"Are we still engaged?"

"Not for long."

"Well, okay, then." He started the engine again and continued down the road. It took two miles for him to fully process her words. "Just out of curiosity, what do you mean by 'sort of' and 'not for long'?"

"It means we have to take a short detour on the way home."

"Where?"

She swallowed. "Reno, Vegas, or Lake Tahoe. Our choice."

Swearing more virulently, Luc swerved into a dirt lane and killed the engine. "What. Did. You. *Do?*"

"You don't understand." The words escaped in a rush.

"Explain it to me so I will."

"You remember that gossip magazine that caused so much trouble for your cousins? *The Snitch?*"

"Unfortunately. What's that got to do with us?"

"Well, they somehow got hold of the story that we eloped. I have no idea how it happened," she hastened to add.

"Let me take a wild guess here. Which of your sisters is the most broke?"

"Vida, but—"

"Then that's my guess."

"My sister wouldn't . . ." She hesitated, her brows pulled together and she altered course. "That's not really the point. *The Snitch* is going to print the story in the morning. Primo said that if we don't marry immediately, it will have a serious effect on my future at Bling. That I'll lose the respect of both employees and customers."

Luc grimaced. He wished he could refute his grandfather's claim, but he couldn't. He had a feeling his grandfather had it exactly right, and if their suspicions about Conway Billings were correct, Cousin Connie would be all over this news and use it to Téa's disadvantage. With each new revelation, Luc could feel the trap tightening around him, edging him deeper and deeper into an inescapable corner.

"Plus," she added in a rush. "There's one other small problem."

"What's the other small problem? I think I can take it. Maybe."

"Primo said if you wish to remain a Dante, you'll marry me. But I don't think he was serious." She turned to him. "Do you?"

"You did meet my grandfather, didn't you?"

"You know I did."

"I think that answers your question." He started the car again and pulled onto the road.

"So what now?" Tea asked tentatively.

"Now, we drive to Lake Tahoe and get married."

They arrived in Nevada by midday and made short work of obtaining the necessary license. Despite the rush and reluctance, Luc insisted they stop at a boutique for more appropriate clothing—a formal suit for Luc, while Téa chose an ivory calf-length skirt and tailored jacket accented with seed pearls. The shop owner suggested a simple Mantilla style veil with embroidered edges that suited her outfit perfectly. A short time later, Téa emerged from the boutique to discover Luc waiting for her, holding a bridal bouquet of multicolored roses in one hand, and a jeweler's box with two plain wedding bands in the other.

They made the short trip to the venue they'd selected and were given the choice of having the ceremony performed in the chapel or in a glorious flower-filled garden just behind the small stucco building. To Téa's surprise, Luc didn't hesitate, but selected the garden. She couldn't help but wonder if he chose it because it reminded him of Primo's backyard.

Both had large, sprawling shade trees and well-tended flower beds, bursting with a riot of colors. They took their vows beneath an arching arbor draped with deep red roses that filled the air with their lush scent. Twenty short minutes later they were pronounced husband and wife.

Téa didn't recall much of the drive back to San Francisco. She knew they kept the conversation light and casual. But she had no idea what either of them said. Awareness returned when Luc bypassed the turn for

Madam's row house and continued on toward his apartment.

"Aren't you going to drop me off at home?"

He glanced in her direction. "Why would I do that? We're married, remember?" he asked with devastating logic. "I think your grandmother and stepsisters would find it extremely odd if you spent your wedding night under their roof instead of mine."

She blushed, feeling like an utter fool. "Oh. Of course. I didn't think."

Luc parked the rental car, said something about returning it in the morning and grabbed their bags while she gathered up the rest of their paraphernalia. They accomplished the elevator ride to his apartment in strained silence. The minute the doors parted, he carried his duffel through to his bedroom and then put her case just inside the doorway of the spare room.

Message received, loud and clear.

"Would you like a drink?" he offered politely.

She debated, then nodded. "I wouldn't say no to a glass of wine."

"Red?"

"Please." He poured her a glass and then fixed himself a whiskey. "It's almost identical to the last time I was here," she observed. "Except for the marriage part."

He eyed her broodingly. "That's a big exception."

She gently placed her bouquet on the table beside the couch. The flowers were already beginning to wilt, she realized with a sad pang. It seemed fitting, all things considered. Soon they'd have to return to reality, which meant putting her focus on work and family, while Luc went back to avoiding commitment at all costs. "I know you have something eating at you. Why don't you just say what you need to so we can go to bed?"

"All this worked out to your advantage, didn't it?"

She closed her eyes. She suspected that was what he thought. It hurt to have it confirmed. "You think I set it up, don't you?"

He took a moment to swallow his drink. "The thought crossed my mind."

"Let it uncross your mind," she said sharply. "You said no to marriage. I accepted that. End of story."

"And yet, within hours my ring ended up on your finger."

"Because of your family, Luc. *Yours*. Not mine. Madam was merely disappointed in me.

I could have lived with her disappointment. It was Primo who forced the issue."

"You're forgetting Primo pushed because someone leaked the news to *The Snitch*. There are only a limited number of people who could have done that."

She lifted an eyebrow. "All of whom are de Lucas?"

"Pretty much."

She took a step in his direction. "You always claimed I was a lousy liar. Look at me, Luc. Hear me." She spoke quietly. Forcefully. "I didn't trick you into marrying me. I didn't ask anyone in my family to get in touch with *The Snitch*. I would never do such a thing to you."

He inclined his head. "Fair enough."

"Do you believe me?" she pressed.

"I believe you."

"But you still want someone to blame."

"Yes. No." He released his breath in a sigh. "I'm as much to blame as anyone."

"Thank you for that much," she said dryly.

"I want you to understand something, Téa." His eyes glittered darkly, with just a hint of gold. "This doesn't change anything."

"What do you mean?"

"You know what I mean. This is temporary. In a few months I plan to walk away."

"I know." And she did. She'd just hoped . . . She set her glass down, exercising extreme care. "I don't think I want a drink after all. I'm exhausted. If you don't mind, I'll turn in."

He stopped her as she started from the room. Just a brush of his fingers along her arm. "Téa . . ."

The Inferno stirred, flared to life, sizzling and crackling with unmistakable urgency. She longed to turn and step into his arms. To beg him to allow her in. To give her a chance. "Don't. I can't—" She shook her head, struggling for control. "Please, don't."

Without another word, he let her go.

She got ready for bed, moving mindlessly through her nighttime regimen. At long last, she slid between the sheets and curled into a ball. Just a few short hours ago she'd been married. This was her wedding night. Never in her wildest dreams had she imagined she'd spend it alone. Or that the man she married would have given almost anything to rip the ring from his finger, and her from his life.

Tears burned against her eyelids, slipped out and left scalding streaks down her cheeks. She buried her face in the pillow, fighting not to make any sound as she cried. She never heard the door to her room open. Never heard Luc limp across the floor. One minute, she huddled in her bed, the next she curled against his chest as he lifted her and carried her to his room.

"What are you doing?" she choked out the question.

"It's my wedding night," he said, echoing her earlier thoughts. "And I'll be damned if I'm going to spend it alone."

He deposited her in his bed, then joined her there. In the silence of the night, he gathered her up. Her nightgown whispered away, melting into the darkness. Then his hands found her. Stroked her. Spoke the words he refused to. With every touch, every caress, he gave of himself, allowing what he guarded so carefully free rein.

Where before they came together in clashing power, now they gently slid, one into the other. Sweetly. Tenderly. The climax, when it came, was every bit as powerful, but it contained a different quality. A need answered. Two hearts united. A consummation of not just bodies, but of souls.

Just before sleep consumed her, he wrapped her up in his arms, hands intertwined, palms meshed. From a great distance she heard his whisper. "Good night, my Inferno bride."

"Good night, my Inferno husband," someone answered. Not her. It couldn't have been her. "Oh, Luc. I do love you."

When Tea awoke, she was alone in the bed.

A quick search of Luc's apartment confirmed he'd gone, though the scent of freshly brewed coffee drew her to the kitchen. Beside the pot, she found a note that read: *Don't go in to Bling until I get back.* The word "don't" was underlined several times. It took two cups of coffee to figure out why. If she planned to oust her cousin and assume the reins of Billings, she'd better do it with a plan. Because, guaranteed, Connie had one.

After a quick shower, she ate breakfast and drafted a press release announcing the change in management, fussing over each and every word, striving to get it just right. It took several hours to perfect. She'd just finished when Luc returned. He was accompanied by a tank-size black man whom he introduced as Juice.

She offered her hand, amused when it got swallowed up in his. "Pleased to finally meet you," he said. "Luc's had a lot to say about you."

"Some of it good, I hope."

"Good enough to make me wonder why you'd waste your time on him when I'm available."

She grinned. "Maybe if I'd met you first . . . ?"

He waggled his eyebrows at her. "You'd be counting your lucky stars and singing praises on high."

"If you're done hitting on my wife," Luc interrupted, "I'd like to give her an update."

Téa buried a smile. "I just brewed a fresh pot of coffee. I drank the last one while drafting a press release."

"You read my mind."

Once everyone had fresh coffee, they gathered at the dining room table. Luc took the lead. "First, let's deal with the issue of the new equipment Conway has been purchasing. FYI, Juice was my top researcher when I owned my own security business before he came to work at Dantes as our head of security. He was able to locate where Connie had the equipment stashed."

"How did you do that?" Téa asked in amazement.

"Uh . . ." Juice darted Luc a panicked look. "Best if I don't tell you. It's not exactly leg— That is to say . . ."

"It's none of your business," Luc cut in. "We also have temporarily relocated said equipment. My men should be finished moving it by noon."

"Wait a minute. You stole Connie's machinery?"

The two men exchanged glances. "Well, technically, it belongs to Billings since he used company money to purchase it," Luc explained. "Which means it's yours to move if you want. I merely decided that's what you wanted and acted on it."

"Of course." She didn't know why it hadn't occurred to her first. "Will that be sufficient to keep him from starting up a competing business?"

"That's the hope."

Téa nodded in satisfaction. "Then the next step is to get Connie out with as little fuss as possible while keeping our current customers." She put the press release she'd drafted on the table. "See what you think about this."

Luc and Juice scanned it. "Oh, Connie's not going to be happy," Luc said, with a merciless grin. "Particularly when he reads the part about being a distant relative of your grandfather who, quote, has been forcibly removed as CEO for failing to maintain Billings' high standard of producing top quality merchandise, which is the number one priority for Daniel Billings'

212 | P a g e

granddaughter, the company's new CEO. End quote." He shoved the release back across the table toward her. "One major error."

Téa snatched up the paper. "What? Where?"

"Your name. It says Téa de Luca. It should say Téa Dante."

The correction brought tears to her eyes. Considering how he felt about their marriage, it meant the world to her he'd insist she use the Dante name. "Silly of me," she murmured. "I'll change it right away."

Luc nodded in satisfaction. His cell rang just then. "Yes, Sandford," he said, leaving the table to take the call. "What did you find out?"

It took Téa a moment to place the name, but then she remembered the deputy who'd been so helpful after their car crash. She only caught snatches of Luc's conversation, but when he returned a grim fury clung to him. He gave Juice a nod before turning to Téa.

"Let's go," he announced. "Time for you to kick Cousin Connie to the curb."

Chapter Ten

Conway Billings didn't take kindly to being kicked to the curb.

Téa swept into his office without bothering to knock, followed closely by Luc and Juice. Conway looked up, his face darkening in outrage. "What the hell do you mean by waltzing in here without permission? You may take over in another month, Téa, but until then this is still my office."

"You're mistaken, Connie. It's now my office." She took a stance in front of his desk, her hands planted on her hips. "And don't call me Téa. The name is Mrs. Dante."

Her cousin's mouth opened and closed several times. "When . . . ?"

She lifted an eyebrow. "Did I get married? Luc and I were married yesterday."

"Yesterday? I . . . You . . ." He resorted to bluster. "You were supposed to be getting to know our clients. How are you ever going to learn what you need to—"

"That's no longer your concern," she interrupted. "As of this minute, you're no longer in charge."

"There's still another month until it's official, Téa." Luc and Juice both took a single step forward and Conway's eyes bulged. *Mrs. Dante,*" he hastened to correct. "You don't take possession of Billings until next month."

"I suggest you go back and reread the will, Connie." She circled the desk, putting herself on his side of it. Then she edged her hip onto the corner in a decidedly possessive maneuver. "In case you overlooked it, I also take possession of the company the day I marry. Since that happy event took place yesterday, I'm now the new owner of Billings."

"Don't be ridiculous, Te—" a quick look at Luc "—*Mrs. Dante*. You're not ready to assume control."

"That's quite possible. Time will tell. What I can say with absolute certainty is that you're through. I have security waiting outside the door. They'll escort you off the premises."

His breath hissed in surprise. "What's brought this on?" His gaze shot to Luc and narrowed. "He's responsible for this, isn't he?"

"No, Connie," she corrected very gently. "You are. Did you think I wouldn't figure it out?"

He stiffened. "Figure what out?"

"The equipment. Billings Prime. I did get the name right, didn't I? That's what you plan to call your new company?"

His chin shot up, his jowls wobbling. "I have no idea what you're talking about."

"Stop. I uncovered it all. The way you cut corners to save money and churn out inferior merchandise. The business you planned to start up. The new manufacturing equipment you bought with the extra profits you gained from overcharging my customers. How you planned to use the drop in quality to convince those same customers to switch to Billings Prime. The sale you're currently drafting so your company can buy the new manufacturing equipment from Billings for only pennies on the dollar. That was particularly slick, Connie."

"And if I did all that, so what?" He shoved back his chair, fury reddening his face. "This should have been my company! I worked here my entire life." He didn't bother to conceal his disgust. "You're not even a Billings. You gave up your rights to this company when you let de Luca adopt you."

She straightened, faced him down. "That decision was my grandfather's to make. Obviously, he didn't agree with you since he left Billings to me, not you." She tilted her head to one side. "I wonder why that is? He must have figured you out long ago."

Conway smoothed the front of his suit jacket and drew himself up to his full height, as little as it was. "It's too late for you to do anything about it. That equipment now belongs to me. I wasn't planning to bring Billings Prime online for another month, but I won't have any difficulty moving up my agenda."

"I think you'll not only find that difficult, but impossible," Téa replied. "I rescinded the sale of the manufacturing equipment between Billings and Billings Prime first thing this morning and I've confiscated that equipment. All you have left is a name. No equipment, no merchandise to sell, and when my press release hits, not much of a reputation, either."

"That's impossible! I'll . . . I'll sue."

"I wish you would." She smiled coldly. "But I doubt you will, considering when all the facts are brought to light, you'll most likely find yourself sitting in a jail cell."

Luc stepped forward. "And if by some chance the judge is inclined toward leniency, it won't last long. Not when he discovers you ordered her to take that trip to L.A. Then Monday you arranged to have her brakes tampered with while her car was parked in Billings' garage. No doubt you were hoping the results would be a one-way trip." He shook his head, every harshly carved inch of his face betraying both fury and ruthlessness. "No, I wouldn't expect any leniency at all."

Téa swung around to face her husband. She didn't even attempt to conceal her shock. "What?"

"Deputy Sandford called. Someone mixed transmission fluid in with your brake fluid. It's slower than simply cutting the lines. No doubt he wanted to give you plenty of time to get on some of the more treacherous stretches of road before your brakes went out. Might have worked, too."

Téa fought to breathe. "It would have worked if you hadn't been driving."

She turned to face her cousin. She saw his mouth moving, could hear denials spilling out. But her brain couldn't seem to process them. Instead guilt burned like acid in his unrepentant blue eyes.

"I want him out of here," she said, her voice cutting through whatever her cousin was saying. It took every ounce of self-control to keep from physically attacking him. He must have sensed it because he fell back as she approached. "Just so you know, Connie? Just so it's crystal clear. My sisters will inherit the business if anything happens to me. And every last scrap of information my husband has uncovered about your activities is going to be turned over to the appropriate authorities. I suggest you find yourself a good lawyer."

"Screw finding a lawyer," Luc said. "Find yourself a nice, deep hole, *Cuz*. Somewhere I won't find you. Because if I ever see you again, I swear I'll take you apart."

Billings' security stepped in then and with Juice's assistance, escorted Conway out of the office, out of the building—and she sincerely hoped—out of her life. The instant the door closed behind them, Téa sank into the chair behind Connie's—*her*—desk.

"That's that," she murmured.

Luc inclined his head. "You're now the boss. Congratulations."

A tiny frown tugged at her brow. "Thanks to you."

"Happy to help." He shoved his hands into his trouser pockets and strolled across the spacious room to stand in front of the windows. "I guess my job is done now."

Maybe if he hadn't said it with such finality, she'd have known how to respond. She hesitated, before conceding, "I guess it is."

He threw her a look over his shoulder. "You okay?"

"Sure. Fine." Only she wasn't. Not even a little.

"Anything else I can do for you?"

Love me. Stay with me. Make our marriage real. She silently shook her head.

"If you're sure, then I'll push off."

"Thanks again for all your help," she managed to say.

For ten minutes after Luc left, Téa continued to sit behind the huge desk, numb. So this was it. In the blink of an eye, he'd given her everything she thought she wanted, and she owed him more than she could ever repay.

Because he suspected her cousin might be attempting something underhanded, he used his time, skill, and associates to look into Connie's background. More, he and Juice uncovered her cousin's plan and moved to circumvent it. And thanks to Luc agreeing to marry her, she'd gained control of her inheritance in time to stop Connie from gutting it. With a lot of hard work and dedication, she'd turn Billings around and salvage her family's finances. But she'd lose something far more important. Luc.

Her mouth trembled. Of course, that was assuming she'd ever had him. She leaned back and closed her eyes, fighting exhaustion. She loved her husband. Loved him with all her heart and soul. Loved him with every fiber of her being. And because she loved him, she'd let him go. Knowing Luc, that wouldn't be easy, despite his aversion toward marriage. She'd need to prove she could stand on her own two feet. And she'd have to find a way to get him out of their marriage without his looking like the bad guy.

Unfortunately, she knew precisely how to do it, too. Even more unfortunate, she'd give him up, regardless of the personal cost. She just wished she could offer him something in return to show him how much she appreciated everything he'd done for her.

A light tapping sounded at the door and Juice peeked in. "What happened to Luc?" he asked.

"He's gone." A sudden idea struck her. One final way she could even the scales. She straightened in her chair, energized. "Juice, I wonder if you'd do one more favor for me."

"Sure." He stepped into her office. "Name it."

"There's someone I need you to find."

Luc checked his watch and grimaced. He was late for his dinner date with Téa. Not badly, but more than he liked. Maybe it had been his subconscious way of putting off the inevitable. Because he suspected he knew what she wanted. She wanted to end their marriage so she could return to her default setting—taking care of her family. Of course, he wanted to end their marriage, too. No long-term commitments for him. He'd made that abundantly clear.

So, why the reluctance?

It couldn't have anything to do with those words she'd whispered on their wedding night. Words that burned a path straight to his heart. Words he wasn't even sure she remembered speaking. Words that confessed how much she loved him. For some reason they resonated, wrapped around him, through him, binding them as surely as the itch in his palm bound them.

"Luc Dante," he practically growled at the maître d'. "I'm meeting someone."

"Yes, Mr. Dante. She's already arrived. I'll show you to your table." He gestured toward the interior of the restaurant. "This way."

Luc followed the winding pathway through the various tables to a small alcove where a woman waited. It took an instant to realize that she wasn't Téa. The maître d' made a flourishing gesture, then retreated before Luc could explain that he'd been shown to the wrong table. He offered the woman an exasperated smile.

"Sorry about the mistake. I was supposed to meet my wife and—"

"There's no mistake," the woman said. She tilted her head to one side. "You don't recognize me, do you? Would it help if I told you that you saved my life five years ago?"

Luc hesitated and looked more carefully. There was something familiar about her. Then it hit him. The car wreck. Kurt and the Jorgen boy, dead. The wife, pleading, begging him to let her die. *"Sonya?"*

Téa checked her watch and bit down on her lip. Right about now Luc and Sonya Jorgen would be getting reacquainted, assuming Luc stayed to talk after learning that his wife had set him up. A big if. Since she hadn't received an outraged phone call, she could only hope the impromptu meeting yielded positive results instead of it all going hideously wrong. A distinct possibility, she was forced to concede. But if it worked . . . She closed her eyes and fought a rush of tears. If it worked, it would be the first of her parting gifts, gifts she could only pray would pay him back for all he'd done for her. Now for gift number two.

She let herself into the home that until recently she'd shared with Madam and her three sisters. She'd deliberately chosen a time when she was certain they'd all be together. The dinner hour. It was all part of her plan to try to put Luc's life back on track before their divorce. If he no longer had to worry about her, he'd feel free to move on.

She found the de Luca clan in the kitchen, squabbling over dinner preparations. She couldn't help smiling. Some things never changed. It took them a moment to realize she was there. The instant they did, they turned to greet her, the volume going up by several hundred decibels.

"What's for dinner?" she asked with a wide smile. "I'm starving."

"What are you doing here?" Madam demanded. "Where's Luc?"

"He has an appointment this evening, so I thought I'd have dinner with you." She eyed each in turn. "We need to talk."

"Actually," Sonya said, "it's not Jorgen, anymore. It's Thompson."

"You remarried?"

His shock must have shown because she smiled and waved him toward the chair across from her. Once he was seated, she studied him with frank curiosity. "It's been five years and you haven't changed a bit, Luc," she murmured.

"You still have the saddest eyes I've ever seen. You know, it was the first thing I noticed about you."

He took his time replying. "I may not have changed, but you have," he surprised himself by saying. "Your eyes aren't sad at all."

She lit up. "No, I guess they wouldn't be."

She shook out her napkin and spread it across her lap. Luc's gaze followed her movements, dropping downward. He froze. "You're—"

"Pregnant?" she asked with a lilting laugh. "Why, yes, I am."

"What's this about, Téa?" Madam asked apprehensively. "Has something happened between you and Luc?"

"Yes. We're going to be divorcing soon." She held up her hand when everyone began talking at once. "That's enough."

For some reason the quietly spoken words worked, cutting through the cacophony of feminine voices. Odd. It had never worked before. But then, she'd never been this serious or determined before.

"I'm not going to discuss it or answer any questions. I'm just going to say that the relationship didn't work out. As a result, I've decided to make some changes. A lot of changes." She eyed each in turn before settling on Juliann. "I've been a lousy wedding planner, Jules. I'm sorry about that."

"It hasn't been so bad," Juliann instantly denied.

"Yes, it has." Téa reached into her shoulder bag and pulled out the shiny black cell phone with its neon-pink kisses. She placed it on the table. "I appreciate you including me in the preparations, but I think what I'd enjoy most is just being there for you on your special day."

Juliann's eyes misted. "That's all I ever wanted, too. But you've always tried to fill in for Mom, and I figured . . ."

Téa closed her eyes. Of course. "You were trying to let me play the traditional mother role, weren't you?" She blinked back tears and offered her sister a wobbly smile. "Thank you. To be honest, I don't want to be your mother, anymore. But I'd love to be your sister."

For some reason, her confession caused all her sisters to tear up. Then there were hugs all around before Davida said, "I gather I'm next?"

"Yes," Téa confirmed. She nudged the phone farther away. "Stay in college or don't. It's your decision. But I'm not bailing you out anymore."

Davida nodded. "You're not going to have to. The professor whose exam I missed? He sat me down and we had a long talk. I realized that what I really want to do is design jewelry. Luc put me in touch with Sev's wife, Francesca. She's going to mentor me while I take the classes I need."

Téa blinked. *"Luc* put you in touch?"

Davida made a face. "I'm sorry you two are getting divorced. I like him. He's nice."

Katrina held out her hand, gloved palm up. "Finish it, Téa. I know it's my turn to get cut off."

Téa slid the phone the rest of the way across the table. "Not cut off, just cut down to reasonable, although I am canceling this line."

"That's okay. And FYI? You don't have to worry about me, either. I've decided I'm going into the military. That or I'm gonna be a cop."

Téa could only stare. "You must be joking," she finally said.

"Nope. I've gotten to know a lot of cops over the past year." She shot Madam a nervous glance. "You know. Community service projects."

Madam simply narrowed her eyes at her granddaughter and let it pass.

"Anyway, it got me interested in law enforcement." Katrina lounged back in her chair and lifted a pierced eyebrow. "So, we done?"

Madam cleared her throat. "You . . . you haven't mentioned me," she said with heart-wrenching dignity. "You may give me my phone, too, if you wish."

Téa hastened to her grandmother's side and enfolded her in a tight hug. "Never. I'll always be there for you." She looked at her sisters and, in that moment, finally forgave herself for her parents' death. "I'll always be there for all of you. But as a sister. As a granddaughter."

Madam dabbed at her eyes. "I think that can be arranged."

Luc was surprised to discover he enjoyed the hour he spent with Sonya. "I assume Téa arranged this?" he said, taking a not-so-wild guess.

"Your wife? Yes. Such a lovely woman. She tracked me down and explained that you were still dealing with the aftermath of what happened all those years ago." Remorse swept across Sonya's face. "I'm so sorry, Luc. I'd give anything to take back those hideous things I said to you. I was out of my mind with grief."

"I understood." He tossed some money into the billfold the waiter had left and set it to one side. "I never blamed you."

Sonya's mouth twisted. "I'm not so sure. That's why I jumped at the opportunity to meet with you, so I could thank you."

"Thank me?" Of all the things he'd imagined her ever saying to him, this was bottom of the list. Hell, it didn't even make the list.

She pushed aside her decaf coffee, picking her words with care. "I was so angry with you, Luc. I wanted to die and you forced me to live. I hated you for that. I even attempted to commit suicide. Did you know?" At his silent nod, she shrugged. "Somehow I'm not surprised. Afterward, much to my amazement, I realized I no longer wanted to die. It took time and a lot of counseling, but I discovered I had a very simple choice. I could open myself up to love again, or continue to live a barren life. When I chose to open up, I found love." A radiant smile played at the corners of her mouth. "Actually, I found my soul mate."

"I thought that was Kurt," Luc said, startled.

"So did I. I was wrong," she replied simply. "What I loved about my life with Kurt was being married. What I loved was—" Her voice broke. "My son. I still miss him, Luc. I'll always miss him. But I can and will honor his memory by moving on and giving him brothers and sisters.

He may never know them, but they'll always know him. I'll see to that."

Luc's jaw clenched and it took him a minute before he could speak. "I'm glad you made it through. That you found love again."

"You can, too." She leaned forward, speaking with a hushed intensity. "I'm reading between the lines here, but don't make the mistake I almost did. Don't turn away from life. Take the gamble, Luc, before it passes you by. Everyone experiences heartache. But that's going to happen whether you're alone or with someone you love. It's love that gets you through. Téa strikes me as a woman who can both fill your life with love, and be strong enough to ride out the heartache with you."

A short time later, Luc climbed into his car. He didn't bother to start the engine, but simply sat, mulling over the events of that evening. It occurred to him that when he saved Sonya, he'd given her back her life, but had shut down his own. She was right about a lot of things. He did have a choice. He could continue on as he had before Téa tumbled into his life or he could take a chance. He could open his heart and take the risk.

He thought about his grandparents and nearly sixty years of profound love and devotion, laughter and tears. It was the same with his parents. With his cousins. Would they avoid love if it meant avoiding the tears? He didn't even have to think about that one. They'd choose love every time.

He considered what his life would be like if he moved forward without Téa. Losing her warmth and generosity. Her humor and passion. God help him, her love. And he remembered her murmured declaration on their wedding night and felt something hard and cold begin to loosen and break.

It was the ultimate gamble. Either he loved Téa and wanted to spend the rest of his life with her, was willing to open himself to her in every possible way. Or he let her go. Watched from afar as she moved on and found someone else to love. Someone else to give all that she'd given him.

He shook his head. *No.* No way in hell. As though in reaction, his palm itched and he stared at it. He was an idiot. He'd turned away from the best, most important parts of his life. And why? Because he'd been too much of a coward to take a risk. Well, screw that! It was past time that he took back his life. That he went after what he wanted most.

And what he wanted most was Téa, the woman he loved with all his heart and soul. His Inferno soul mate.

Before he could start the engine, his cell phone rang. He checked the caller ID and flipped it open. "What's up, Nonna?"

She spoke in rapid-fire Italian. "Your wife is here," she said without preamble. "You must come. Now."

He shot up in his seat. "What's wrong?"

"Téa is explaining to Primo why your marriage is a mistake. That he must not interfere in the divorce. What is this talk of a divorce, *cucciolo mio?*" she demanded. "You have only just married."

Hell. "Has Primo taken her apart, yet?"

"No, no. He is being very patient. Very understanding." His grandmother sighed. "She is a determined one, though, that wife of yours. Determined to get her head handed to her."

"Nonna, I need you to do me a favor."

"Anything."

"Break out Primo's homemade beer and stall." He cut the connection and immediately dialed Sev. "I need you to meet me at the Dante vault. Yes, now. She's what? Hell. Well, can you meet me on the way to the hospital? You're damn right it's an emergency. It's a matter of life and . . . And love."

Téa blinked owlishly at Primo and waved her bottle of beer at him. So far, her third gift to Luc wasn't going so well. At this rate, she'd never even up those scales. "So, you understand, right?" she asked hopefully.

Primo slanted a look in Nonna's direction, gritted his teeth and said, "Maybe if you explain one more time?"

"Oh." She suppressed a burp and lifted a hand to her aching head. "To be honest, I'm not sure I can."

"Good. We talk of other things now, yes? How do you like babies?" he asked expansively. "You and Luc will make many good babies. Inferno babies with red Inferno hair, okay?"

Téa sniffed. For some reason his question had tears welling up in her eyes. "Haven't you been listening? There aren't going to be any babies."

He leaned back in his chair and grinned. "There are always babies when your husband is a Dante." He fixed his attention on a spot over her shoulder. "Is this not true, Luciano?"

"Absolutely, Primo."

Téa swung around and almost fell off her chair. "Oh, dear," she murmured as the room did a slow 360 around her.

"How many?" Luc asked Nonna with a sigh.

His grandmother shrugged. "Three or four."

"Maybe five," Primo offered helpfully.

"Damn. I was hoping she'd remember tonight."

"I'll remember tonight," Téa protested. "Why won't I remember?"

Luc tipped her face up to his. "Because, darling wife," he said, enunciating carefully. "You're drunk."

"Am not."

He gave his grandfather a stern look. "Coffee and lots of it. In the meantime . . ." He swept his wife into his arms. "Let's hope some fresh air will do the trick. By the way, you might want to give Sev a call. Francesca's in labor and they're on their way to the hospital."

Téa tipped her head back as Luc carried her into the garden. A dazzling canopy of stars glittered and burned like Dantes legendary fire diamonds. Cool spring air swirled around and over her in soft revitalizing currents. It helped clear her head and she stirred, suddenly aware that she'd somehow ended up where she most longed to be—in Luc's arms.

"Where did you come from?" she asked dreamily. "Or am I just imagining you?"

"Oh, I'm real enough," he claimed.

Not that she believed him. Having him here like this was just too good to be true. "This is so nice." Since he was a dream, she could indulge herself and she scattered her kisses across his bronzed skin, like the stars scattered their dust across the heavens. "We can pretend to still be married and have another glorious wedding night."

He smiled with breathtaking tenderness. "We don't need to pretend. We are still married."

"Not for long."

"True. Only a half dozen decades or so."

She laughed. "Now I know I'm dreaming."

He lowered her to a wrought iron bench situated beneath one of Primo's shade trees. The cold metal brought her surroundings into sharp focus. Luc really was here. And he really was holding her in his arms.

"Seriously," she said, her brain slowly coming online. "What are you doing here?"

"I wanted to thank you for arranging the meeting with Sonya tonight."

Sonya? Her brow crinkled. Oh! *Sonya.* "I was afraid you might be angry with me," she confessed.

"Not even a little."

"I'm so glad. I asked Juice to help me find her." She nestled against him, resting her head in the crook of his shoulder, allowing herself this one final indulgence. "How did it go?"

"She's remarried, but I guess you knew that." At Téa's nod, he added, "And she's pregnant."

Téa looked up at Luc, startled. "Is she really? That's good, right?"

"It's very good. She was ecstatic."

"Pregnant." Téa frowned. "Wait a minute. Did I hear you tell your grandparents that Francesca was in labor, or did I dream that part?"

"It wasn't a dream. She's in labor and Sev isn't very happy with me."

"Why ever not?"

"Because I made him stop off at the Dantes vault on the way to the hospital."

"I'm confused," Téa confessed with a sigh. "And it's all Primo's fault."

"Nonna's, actually. I told her to feed you beer until I got here."

It took all her courage to ask. "Why?"

"So I could give you this."

He held out a small jewelry box and flipped open the lid. Inside was nestled the most beautiful ring she'd ever seen, with a platinum gold band, Billings gold, Téa realized, a type her grandfather had dubbed, Platinum Ice. The band took the shape of two hearts linked together with a magnificent fire diamond set where the hearts joined.

It took several tries before she could speak. "I don't understand."

"I love you, Téa. And I want a real marriage. A permanent one."

"No," she whispered, shaking her head. "That's not what you want. You want to be apart. Alone."

"I was wrong. I can't live like that. Not anymore. Not since meeting you." She watched as he struggled to find the right words, to open himself in a way he never had before. "I can't promise I'll be perfect at it. I've spent a lot of years holding people at an emotional distance. But for you I'm willing to give everything I have. And with luck, we'll spend the rest of our lives getting it right."

"Oh, Luc. I came here to let you go." She gazed in the direction of the house and fought an onslaught of tears. "But I couldn't get your grandparents to listen to me. To understand and let you off the hook."

"Because they knew you were the one. My Inferno bride."

His admission melted her. "I love you so much, Luciano Dantes."

"And I love you, Téa, more than I ever thought possible. My life would be empty without you and I think I've had all the emptiness I can bear." He slid the ring on her finger. It fit perfectly. But then, he knew it would. It was destiny. "It's from our new line of eternity rings. It has a name, if you're interested. It's actually the reason I chose it."

It took her two tries to get the question out. "What's the name?"

He lowered his mouth to hers. "Why, Dante's Inferno, of course."

Epilogue

Nonna touched her wineglass to Madam's. *"Salute."*

Madam smiled tremulously. "We did it, didn't we?"

Nonna eyed Luc and Téa with smug satisfaction. "That we did. Of course, it was your managing to accomplish Step Two that allowed Primo to insist on Step Three." She released a contented sigh. "And that just leaves Step Four."

"Step Four?" Madam's eyes widened in concern. "What step is this?"

"Babies. More precious Dante babies. Boys for these two." Nonna lifted her glass in the direction of her grandson. "But that I will leave to Luc. I believe he has the matter well in hand."

From his position at the kitchen window, Rafe Dante regarded Luc and his bride, Téa, with a cynical smile. They were in Primo's garden, enjoying the party thrown to celebrate their elopement, and accepting the congratulations of all the well-wishers. Babies abounded: one from Francesca, as well as Kiley's contribution. Both sons, of course. The two mothers were comparing everything from birthing experiences to feeding schedules. Hell, they were even comparing toes.

To Rafe's amusement, Luc looked on, taking an actual interest. Unheard of! But then, his poor brother was the latest victim of The Inferno. Of all the Dantes, Rafe had always figured that he and Luc were the two least likely to ever succumb to the family plague. For some reason, it made him feel fiercely alone. Which was the way he wanted it, right? God knows, Leigh had caused him enough heartache that he never wanted to give another woman that much power over him. But watching his family . . .

He deliberately turned away.

Luc joined him midway through the festivities, taking the tumbler of whiskey Rafe offered. "I hear we've been cleared to return to work."

"As of today," Rafe confirmed. "Dantes Courier Service reopens first thing Monday morning. You coming back?"

"You couldn't keep me away."

Rafe nodded in satisfaction. "Congratulations, by the way. Téa's a beautiful woman." He paid the compliment with complete sincerity. "You're a lucky man." Okay, maybe that wasn't quite as sincere.

"Yes, I am," Luc agreed. He fixed Rafe with a speculative eye. "I know you're one of the unbelievers."

"Check mark firmly in that column," Rafe confirmed.

"I guess we have Leigh to thank for that." Luc rested his hip against the kitchen counter. "Tell me something. Did you believe in The Inferno when you first fell in love with her? When the two of you first married?"

Rafe took a long swallow of his drink. "What makes you think that?'"

Luc froze. "Wait a sec. You didn't feel . . . ?" He rubbed his palm.

"Don't be ridiculous. Of course not."

Luc straightened. "Are you telling me you never felt The Inferno for Leigh?"

Rafe released an incredulous laugh. "You're as crazy as the rest of them. Don't you get it? There is no Inferno."

Luc simply smiled.

A hint of anger ripped through Rafe. "Don't. Don't give me that smug, knowing look. You and the rest of our deluded relatives fell in love. That's all there is to it. But because of our family's ridiculous myth, you're calling this emotion that has you drooling all over your bride The Inferno. Well, I've got news for you, brother. It's illogical. Not to mention messy." He leaned forward, speaking distinctly. "In my book that means The Inferno doesn't exist."

"I'm sure that explains the itch," Luc said, straight-faced.

"That itch is called lust. Now, you want to talk lust?" Rafe downed the rest of his drink. "Happy to oblige. Been there, sated that. Moved on."

This time Luc didn't bother to conceal his grin. "Keep talking, Rafe. And keep telling yourself you're immune. But I'm giving you fair warning. Clearly Leigh wasn't the right woman."

Rafe lifted an eyebrow. "You think?"

"You're missing the point. If Leigh wasn't the one, that means your Inferno bride's still out there. And when you find her, you'll know." Luc jabbed his index finger against his brother's chest. "Then we'll see who has the last itch, pretty boy."

The Dante Inferno continues with Rafe's story!

Rafe's Temporary Wife by Day Leclaire

Meet Day Leclaire

I love family first and foremost, which is why writing a family saga is so much fun. Maybe you can tell that from my books since they always feature the warmth and joy that comes from having a close-knit family. I also love animals and have taken in rescue dogs and cats and fostered dogs for the local animal shelter. And of course, I love writing. All I need is a functioning brain (batteries not included), a pen, and paper, and I can write anywhere. Please don't let a conversation with me lag because my imagination takes over and I. Am. Checked. Out!

USA Today bestselling author, Day Leclaire is the author of more than 60 novels and has received an impressive eleven nominations for the romance industry's most prestigious award, Romance Writers of America RITA© Award. Day lives in Charlotte, NC and spends her days obsessively writing while vaguely remembering to pay attention to her adorable husband, busy son and daughter-in-law, two tiny grandchildren, and two even tinier Teddy Bear dogs. Not to mention a whole lot of dust!

Thank you so much for taking the time to read **The Dante Inferno:** *The Dante Dynasty Series*. I hope you enjoy this very special Italian-American family. I love hearing from my readers. For a personal response, please contact me at Day@DayLeclaire.com. And be sure to visit my website at www.DayLeclaire.com. Sign up for my newsletter for my latest releases and insider info available nowhere else! Just visit: https://www.dayleclaire.com/join-my-mailing-list

You can also find me on Facebook at www.facebook.com/Day.Leclaire.Private and Twitter at www.Twitter.com/DayLeclaire.